# LOST LOVE

ELITE MEN OF MANHATTAN BOOK 3

MISSY WALKER

Copyright © 2022 by Missy Walker

All rights reserved.

No part of this publication may be reproduced, distributed or transmitted in any form or by any means, including by any electronic or mechanical means, including photocopying, recording or information storage and retrieval systems, without prior written consent from the author, except for the use of brief quotations in a book review.

Cover Design: Missy Walker

Editor: Swish Design & Editing

*To my girls, follow your heart. When that leads you into doubt and fear, lean in and listen closer.*

# 1
## CONNOR

She was drunk.
*Perfect.*
I never said I was a saint. Far from it. I'd fucked my way through most of Manhattan, and I wasn't ashamed of it. Women swarmed around me like moths to a flame. Who was I to deprive them?

With my back against the wall, I watched her. Pepper Little swayed to the DJ's beat, her hourglass curves seductively drawing me in.

I'd just learned Pepper and Jake, her long-time boyfriend, had broken up. As of tonight, they were no longer an item, and by the way her eyes zeroed in on mine from across the room, she wanted to forget about him. She was my sister's best friend, but I could forget tonight and give her that, if only for tonight.

I'd never fancied Lourde's best friend. Not like that anyway. Pepper was much younger. Eight years to be exact, at just twenty-three. But I never saw age as a barrier before. She was cool and gorgeous, just not my flavor of gorgeous—tall, skinny, blonde, and pillows for titties.

Pepper was the opposite, with olive skin, long black curls,

and dark brown eyes thanks to her Greek roots. She was petite, had curves that wound into a tiny waist and a booty that made both men and women alike turn their heads.

Challenging her to make the next move, I lifted the tumbler to my lips without breaking her gaze. The amber liquid slid down the back of my throat like liquid candy. Her lips peeled upward into a grin before she closed her eyes, letting her hands sink over her scarlet dress, then ran them over the curves of her breasts, down the sides of her body to the swell of her hips. My dick thickened in my pants, watching her touch her body so seductively.

It was only when my sister, Lourde, and her friend, Grace, started dancing next to Pepper did my attention wane, and so did hers.

I wandered back to the bar table where my friends were seated. Ari and Barrett were engaged in conversation while Magnus stared at me like I had two heads.

*Had he seen me gawking at Pepper?*

Lightheadedness and haze swept throughout my six-foot-three frame, and I steadied myself, putting my arm against the wall. It took an awful lot to get me drunk, but clearly, tonight, I was reaching that threshold.

Along with the last few weeks, I'd been giving an alcoholic cause for pause with the amount of alcohol I'd been consuming. It made me forget about what was coming—my future obligations as an heir to a billion-dollar media empire and an arranged marriage decided for me at an early age.

Alfred—who I stopped calling Dad since I could remember — was about to step down as the President of Diamond Incorporated, which meant it was my turn to step in. Not only into a position and responsibility I didn't want but with the announcement of my arranged marriage to Francesca, the daughter of the Duke and Duchess of Cavendish.

With the new role came the impending jail sentence to her.

Okay, maybe, a jail sentence was a slight stretch. She was gorgeous. My fake type of beautiful and not too bad of a fuck, either. But that was it. She was blander than a cracker, and oftentimes, I found the ground more appealing when she spoke.

The alcohol numbed the pain, and after the week of hell my father had put me through as Vice President, I needed to let off some steam.

"Where did you go, man?" Ari slapped me between the shoulders, nearly sending me off balance.

"Noo... wherrre." *Did that come out in a slur?*

"I think you better hold back on the booze," Ari cautioned, moving the bottle of Hennessy closer to him.

"What the fuck, Ari?"

"Hey, man. Just trying to help is all."

"It's a party, lighten up," I snapped, grabbing the bottle from his claw-like grip.

"Man, you've got a set of balls," Magnus said to Ari, his eyebrows raised in disbelief.

"Hey, bud, we're all concerned, that's all," Barrett reassured.

"I'm fine," I leveled back, but looking around the table, all I saw was concern on my friends' faces.

"Geez! All right, here," I conceded, sliding it back across the bar table. "Take the fucking bottle. Now, will you leave me the fuck alone?" I questioned with an over-the-top hand gesture that nearly sent me tumbling over my own feet.

"Jesus fuck, Connor." An arm circled my back, propping me back upright. Blinking a few times, I tried to regain my composure and shake off the umbrella of haze.

"See, I'm fine." I straightened. "Now, who's getting laid? Magnus, since your wife cheated on you, you up?" I gloated like the drunk dick I was.

"Connor, that's low." Magnus narrowed his eyes, his tone clipped.

Fuck, what did he expect marrying a prom queen who had decided the handyman was a better option three months into the marriage?

"I think we need to get you some water." Ari pressed his arm around my shoulder, dragging me toward the bar. Reluctantly, I went, casting my gaze toward Lourde's living room turned dance floor.

If I couldn't drink my distraction, at least there was Pepper. A younger guy hovered crazy close to her body, wriggling his way into her space and wrapping his arms around her waist. Clean-cut, fresh-faced, and a younger version of myself, he was a distraction, nonetheless, but an annoying one at that.

Approaching the bar, Ari signaled the bartender, who was distracted by a busty redhead. "Water, thanks."

I let out a groan.

"You'll thank me when tomorrow rolls around," Ari said. "You know I love you like a brother, man, we all do. But this has got to stop."

I rolled my eyes. "What are you, my dad?"

"No, and if Alfred saw you, he'd send you on a one-way ticket to rehab."

"Yeah, well, fuck him," I spat out just as the bartender slid across the ice water.

"Thanks." Ari nodded, grabbing the glass and shoving it into my chest.

"Drink this, and go home. Sleep it off," he said and walked toward our table. Magnus hovered over to a nearby girl, and Barrett had disappeared.

I gulped down the water, slamming down the empty glass as the bartender watched on. All the while, I couldn't keep my eyes off Pepper. Thankfully, Lourde had disappeared, so now it was time to go over and see exactly how much she wanted to forget about her ex. She would not be doing so with the guy currently pawing at her if I had anything to say about it.

Pushing through the crowd of people, I found my way toward Pepper. His hands were now on her body, sliding around her waist, and my skin bubbled with rage, watching him touch her.

I towered over her petite frame as I approached her. The scent of orchids and roses invaded my senses, and I couldn't stop myself from breathing deeply.

When she looked up at me and I stared down, her delicious tits caught my eye before I met her gaze again.

"What is it, Connor?" She placed both hands around the guy's neck like my presence meant nothing to her.

*Had she done that on purpose? Little did she know it took a hell of a lot to scare me off.*

Anyone else would feel self-conscious watching another couple dance, but I didn't give a flying fuck. I didn't give him the time of day as I kept my focus on her. Apparently, it bothered him to some degree, as his attention fell on me.

"Hey, man. Can't you see we're in the middle of something here," he huffed out before immediately recognizing me and lowering his arms. His posture stiffened.

Ignoring him, I whispered in her ear, "So no Jake then?"

She peeled her arms away from the guy, and he grumbled out something inaudible over the reverberating bassline.

"There are a million girls here. Go find another fuck."

Pepper arched a mocha-colored eyebrow and, with a nod of her head, motioned toward the balcony. I followed.

"Was that necessary?" she asked, turning to face me. "I know you're Connor Diamond, but fuck."

*Why did I like the way my name rolled off her tongue?*

"I am Connor Diamond, and I don't give a fuck what anyone thinks of me."

"Hunkholes," she quipped.

"Hunkholes?" I laughed out loud.

"What is it you want, Connor?" she asked, a blush creeping up her exposed chest.

Wearing a red dress with a tight-fitting bodice that pushed her tits up, it was difficult to stop staring. But my manners carved into me since childhood lifted my eyes back up to meet her scowl.

"You."

She laughed. Then when she realized I wasn't joking, she went silent.

"You need to get over the heartache of what's-his-name, and I just need to forget."

"There are a million girls here like you said."

"There are." I glared at her.

"There are," she repeated in a hoarse whisper, and her timbre tone set my dick alight.

"There's also Lourde…" she said, her gaze falling to the floor.

Fuck, my sister could be a problem. But not if it was a one-time thing—which it definitely would be.

"It's one time… I can keep a secret if you can."

Her full lips split into a smile. "Maybe."

"Maybe?" *Well, that wasn't a no.*

"You deaf, rich boy?"

"That depends on how loud you scream, Pepper."

Her mouth fell open, her brown eyes like saucers. She toyed with the end of her black curls that framed her face. "You're a bad boy, Connor."

"And, why do I think you like bad boys?"

Her lips twisted into a smile. "Goodbye, Connor," she said, turning around and heading back inside.

*What the fuck? I think she just rejected me.* No one ever did that. Pepper just became a challenge I couldn't ignore, and it brought a smirk to my face.

As the party kicked on into the early morning hours, I settled around the living room with my friends and sister.

"Have you guys seen Pepper? I thought that wherever she'd gone, she'd be back by now?" Lourde asked.

"I saw her a while ago," Ari said.

"Wasn't she talking with you on the balcony, Connor?" Magnus shot me a look.

"Before, yes." All sets of eyes pointed in my direction, waiting for me to what? Elaborate?

"What? She was upset, telling me about how she split from Jake."

"They split?" Barrett asked, looking confused.

"Yes, they split! What the hell do you care?" I exclaimed, then suddenly all eyes were on me again.

Barrett put his hands up in surrender.

Christ, what the fuck was his deal? A vein ticked in my neck as I looked away for her.

Lourde cleared her throat. "We all thought they were solid. Regardless, she's not picking up her phone. She's not here, and I'm worried."

"I'm sure she's fine, Lourde." I had known Pepper and Grace, her two besties, since elementary school.

No one fucked with Pepper. Maybe that was the feisty Greek in her, but I knew she could handle herself.

"I wouldn't worry, hun. Pepper always finds her way," Grace added, looking like she'd had one too many champagnes.

Only a handful of people remained at the party as final drinks were served.

"Well, this has been fun, sis. I'm happy to see you're all set up here in your new apartment and out of the family home," I gushed, so proud of my sister, who finally stepped out of my parents' shadow.

Lourde sat down next to Grace, who had slumped down

beside her and closed her eyes momentarily. "Thanks, brother. If I'd known living on my own would be this much fun, I would have moved out earlier."

"Have you seen the old ball and chain?" I asked, and we all laughed. The sound causing Grace to open her eyes and perk up a little.

"No, not since I've moved out. I've been working." Lourde smiled at Barrett, and I couldn't tell if she was being polite or extra friendly. Since staying with him in the Hamptons recently, she'd seemed different.

*But fuck, what did I know?* My own life was imploding in front of my very eyes.

"God forbid you would want to walk over to the little company called Diamond Incorporated and help a brother out." I raked a hand through my hair. Pressure was a motherfucker, and it was squeezing me, slowly choking the life from me.

"I didn't know you needed help, Connor." Her voice was soft, laced with concern, and instantly I felt remorse.

"I don't need any help, Lourde." I pushed off the couch to stand. "Anyway, it's late. I'm calling it a night."

"Really?" Ari asked.

"Yes," I snapped.

"Nah." Magnus folded back into the couch and picked up his beer, taking a sip.

Ari, Magnus, and Barrett remained seated and made no move to leave with me. Some fucking friends they were.

"Whatever. See you later." I leaned over, kissed Lourde on the cheek, and walked toward the elevator, still slightly unsteady on my feet.

I'd made it halfway down the elevator when I remembered I'd left my Hugo Boss jacket hanging off the armchair. Normally, I'd leave it behind, but with a storm rolling in, I'd prefer it on my back.

*Dammit.*

I hit the elevator button with an impatient fist, and the doors closed again. As the elevator shot north, I recalled my earlier argument with Alfred.

*"You're not fit to run my company... but you're my only option seeing we share the same blood."*

I trudged out of the elevator as the door pinged open with renewed irritation. I didn't know why I let him get under my skin. It's not like he was going to change in his old age.

Zeroing in on the armchair where I'd left my jacket, it still hung across the back.

Except something had changed.

Was that the back of Lourde? I walked closer, slower, and in disbelief.

*Fuck me.*

Her head rested on Barrett's shoulder, their shoulders and arms touching.

"What the fuck is going on here?" My voice exploded, cutting through the bass coming through the speakers. Immediately, Barrett moved away from Lourde as she disentangled herself from him.

I heard Ari mumble something, but the pounding of my pulse in my ear was louder.

"Connor, what are you doing back?" Lourde turned to face me, her high-pitched tone revealing her nerves.

"My jacket," I snarled out with a hiss.

I took in Ari and Magnus with Barrett's back still to me. Like two nervous little schoolboys being caught looking through the peephole into the girls' bathrooms, their faces were grim.

*What the actual fuck? Were they a part of this too?*

"I repeat, what the fuck is going on here? Barrett?"

Barrett slowly stood up, turning around so we were at eye level.

My nostrils flared as I sucked back a large intake of oxygen, my body in fight-or-flight mode and positively raging.

"Maybe we should go somewhere more private, Connor," Barrett pleaded.

I stared from Barrett to Lourde, then back around at the lingering people in the apartment who were not so subtly staring our way.

"Fine," I grunted, baring my teeth in barely-there control.

Lourde, who looked like a deer, seconds from being eaten by a lion, now moved to stand next to Barrett.

"Follow me." Lourde motioned toward her bedroom wing.

With each step I took, my body was fueled with more rage, lies, and betrayal.

*What the actual fuck?* What happened in the Hamptons between the two of them? Barrett wouldn't dare.

*Yet tonight, you wanted to fuck Pepper.*

*Hypocrite.*

I shook away the thought.

The door shut behind me, and I faced Barrett, who still had his back toward me.

"Tell me what the fuck is going on because I sure as hell don't think my best friend would be screwing my baby sister."

He walked over to Lourde, standing beside her. She held her hands in front of her, fidgeting with her fingers.

"Look, Connor, we wanted to tell you."

"You fucking what?" Still slightly inebriated, I stepped forward, a bit unsteady on my feet, but before I could reach him, Lourde stepped between us, forcing me to step back.

"Stop it, Connor, and just listen, please."

*Listen, was she fucking serious? My baby sister and Barrett?*

"I love him," she said with her hands on Barrett's chest.

"You fucking what?"

"I love him," she repeated. But her revelation still made no sense the second time.

# Lost Love

Lourde stared at me, then back to Barrett. I was so confused staring between them. What was happening? *Someone, please tell me this was just an alcohol-induced misunderstanding.* That had to be it, *right?*

"It started in the Hamptons when you suggested I stay with him."

Confusion now gave way to intense anger.

I looked past her and squared up to Barrett. "I knew I couldn't trust you. What did I say to you? I said not to fucking touch her." I turned to face Lourde. "He is a player, Lourde. We all are. He's slept with most of Manhattan."

"That was in the past, Connor," Barrett said. "Lourde's different. I've never cared about anyone as much as I do Lourde."

No, this wasn't happening. This wasn't fucking happening in my fucked-up existence.

"You fucking *asshole!*" I leaned over Lourde, grabbing Barrett by the shirt.

Pushing past Lourde, I shoved him against the wall, but he didn't fight me back.

"Stop, please, Connor," Lourde pleaded.

"You can fucking hit me, but you won't stop me from seeing her," he said calm as fuck, and it only pissed me off more.

My hand smashed into the wall next to his head, but again, he didn't flinch.

"You can smash my face up, but she means everything to me, Connor."

Unblinking, he stared back at me. My chest rose and fell sharply as my arm swooped back, ready to strike. Lourde pleaded and said something I couldn't comprehend with the amount of rage building inside of me.

"Fuck you!" I slammed my fist into the wall, this time breaking through the drywall.

"Do it. I'm a piece of shit anyway. I don't deserve your sister."

*The way he looked at her made me think twice. Did he actually have feelings for her?*

I gripped my hand with the other, the pain radiating up my forearm with blood trailing from a cut. Unfortunately, it did nothing to deter the betrayal I felt.

The door swung open. Ari and Magnus looked from him to me, then at the hole in the wall next to Barrett's head.

"Are you all right, Connor?" Ari asked.

"So you all knew too?" I asked, taking the cloth that Lourde passed me to quell the blood dripping from the cuts on my hand.

"I didn't know for sure until I saw them tonight," Magnus said.

"I knew, man, but it wasn't up to me to tell you," Ari admitted, stepping between Barrett and me.

"Is everything all right in here?" Grace asked, taking in the hole in the wall and a shivering Lourde. *Shit, what have I done to my sister?*

Barrett must have noticed her shivering, too, because the next thing I knew, he had moved behind her, wrapping his arms around her.

My jaw ticked with fury, but I remained still. "I'm fucking livid," I said, exasperated. My body vibrated with unreleased tension, and I couldn't stop myself. "No, you know what? I'm fucking furious. How dare you?"

"I'm sorry, Connor. We were going to tell you tomorrow," Lourde said in an anxiety-laden voice.

"He's no good for you, Lourde," I spat out, and Barrett gripped her tighter in response.

"Fuck this," I said. "I can't believe what I'm hearing and seeing. You're eight years younger than him, Lourde."

"I think we all should just go home, regroup with level

heads, and talk about it when we have all calmed down," Magnus said, and maybe it wasn't such a bad idea because I didn't trust myself not to throw a punch at my so-called best friend and follow it with another.

"First the shitstorm with work, and now this? Lourde, seriously..."

"I told you, I'm sorry," Lourde said, stepping out of Barrett's firm grip and toward me.

I saw the pain in her eyes, but it was too much to take. I was fucking angry, and there wasn't a damn thing anyone could do to fix this.

I threw my hands up. "I'm out... and you, Barrett..." I shook my head, my jaw set, glaring at them one last time before turning on my heel toward the door.

"Lourde just happened, Connor," Barrett confessed.

I craned my neck, throwing him a piercing I-don't-give-a-fuck stare, then walked out.

After fending off Magnus and Ari, who followed me out, I left them at Lourde's apartment and pushed them out of the elevator doors.

The elevator descended as I cracked my jaw, grinding my teeth, and as I reached the lobby, anger had utterly consumed me.

The doors opened, and I walked out into a vision of red.

*Pepper.*

## 2

## PEPPER

The elevator doors pinged open, and Connor looked up. The frown etched above his sky-blue eyes was replaced with a fiery stare when his eyes met mine. Mesmerizingly dark with a layer of desperation like he was lost, he halted my movement, and I stopped in my tracks. A fiery warmth climbed my neck while my breath caught in my throat.

He rocked his blue shirt with the sleeves rolled up and tan pants that pressed to his thick thighs. With his height, it was as if he was floating toward me. Or perhaps that was the champagne talking. I couldn't be sure.

"What's wrong, Connor?" I asked, slightly on edge at the intensity of his gaze.

*Did he know about Lourde and Barrett?* It was the first thing that came to mind.

I'd only slightly sobered from the fresh Manhattan air, but I was still hazy from the night's events. Lourde had kept her distance from Barrett all night, *hadn't she?*

He grabbed my hand and pulled me outside. My body responded to his rough and dominant touch, coming alive after being dormant for so long. In Tribeca, where the streetlights glowed and the air was sticky, Connor held onto my wrist.

"What are you doing?" I eventually asked.

He pulled me around the dark corner. I knew Connor wouldn't hurt me, but I knew he was not okay by the force of his hand. My body trembled with anticipation.

"Connor, tell me, what's wrong?"

He pinned me against the brick wall and pressed his body against mine. My back scratched against the roughness in this position, and my heart thundered in my ribcage. Connor's heated stare rendered me speechless. Yet, fear was the last thing running through me. There wasn't anywhere I could go and no place I'd rather be. With his muscles pressed against me, the unspoken promises he could give me flooded my body.

*Oh God.*

Without warning, he slammed his lips against mine in a heated kiss. He tasted of whiskey and sadness. On the tips of my toes, I titled my head up and kissed him back, throwing my hands around his neck. I pulled him closer, wanting his entire body on me.

He groaned in my mouth, then suddenly pulled back. "Not here," he groaned out.

I pulled away breathless to find his pupils dilated, slithers of dark blue surrounded by black.

I wanted him. It was wrong, so very wrong, but I needed to forget my broken heart.

And Connor? Connor was always there.

Familiar.

In the background.

My best friend's older brother.

"Come with me," he commanded, taking my hand and pulling me off the wall.

He hailed a taxi, and on the short ride to his place, his hand discreetly climbed underneath my dress, hovering on the inside of my thigh. He brushed against the lace of my barely-there panties. An indescribable tension pooled inside me, and I couldn't wait to get out of the car to the safety of prying eyes.

As soon as our ride came to a stop, Connor leaped out of the taxi and held out his hand. After he helped me out of the car, his hand slipped from mine as he scanned the area.

We walked side-by-side into the lobby as he greeted the concierge with a polite nod. As soon as the doors closed to the elevator, his hands were on me, biting my shoulder. He inched down my dress, fumbling at the zipper.

"Connor," I breathed out, the rush of blood pooling between my thighs.

Pushing me against the steel elevator rail, he rested his broad shoulders and thick legs against me. Scrambling, I reached for him, wrapping my hands around his neck. As if sensing my struggle, he lifted me onto the rail so my ass balanced between his body and the bar.

Pressed so tightly to me, I felt the tent in his pants, and I sucked in a breath, anticipation shooting between my legs.

"You want this, Pepper?" He stepped back, clutching his cock like a trophy.

It was a question, but there was no inflection in his tone. I knew he wasn't asking. He was Connor Diamond, after all, heir to a billion-dollar media company. Arrogance and entitlement came like cups of tea to the English.

But to me, he was just Connor.

"Fuck, yes," I said, putting my hand on his and squeezing.

He grinned like a schoolboy. "You were always the cheeky one, weren't you?"

"You better believe it," I teased, taking him harder in my hands.

He hissed out a breath.

The elevator doors opened to his penthouse, and he lifted me off the rail with ease, carrying me over the threshold.

I'd been to Connor's apartment many times before with Lourde. I loved his style—homey with a luxurious edge. Warm colors covered custom couches, colorful art dressed the walls, and plush tapestry rugs across the floors felt like clouds underneath your feet. Plenty of wood and lime-washed timber covered the furniture, giving it that warm and inviting feel.

But this was different.

*So different. His hand was on my goddamn ass, for starters, then there was the feel of his hard cock against me.*

When a moment of doubt should have entered my mind, it didn't. Instead, I took my mouth to Connor's exposed neck, sucking it hard.

"Fuck me," he bit out and spanked my ass.

I moaned, wanting him to do it again.

He kicked open the door to his bedroom, and he tossed me onto the bed.

"I want you to wrap your lips around my cock."

My panties were already damp, and his dirty words had me soaked.

He stood at the foot of his king bed and unzipped his pants, springing his enormous erection free. I gasped at the sight. Long, thick, and rod-steel, he was impossibly large.

With a hunger in my eyes, I crawled toward him and licked my lips, unable to wait any longer. The desire to satisfy him, make him forget about whatever was troubling him while making me forget my own heartache was too strong.

"I want to see what's underneath that dress, Pepper," he commanded, roughly chasing down the zipper with expert hands.

His hands circled my breasts encased in my red lace bra in what appeared to be awe, it seemed. God gifted me huge natural tits to go with my round Greek ghetto booty, and at least Connor appreciated them. Then he ripped off the bra from the front, and it split into two, causing my strained breasts to tumble out.

"You didn't like the bra?" I teased.

"Fuck, Pepper, are these natural?"

"All me." I winked.

My hands ached with a need to touch him, and I reached the base of his cock, my fingers closing around him as I stroked his length from base to tip. He let out a guttural groan that sent a throbbing sensation between my legs. How he was this hard, when completely intoxicated, beat me. Jake couldn't even get it up after a few drinks.

His hands traced my tits, squeezing my nipples between his fingers. Hard then soft, he teased me, sending a quiver from my belly down to my core.

Wanting to taste him, I leaned forward, and his hands dropped, giving me permission. I took him in my mouth, and slowly, I licked his tip, moving in a circular motion with long, unhurried strokes.

A raspy moan escaped his lips, and I gazed up, grinning around his cock.

"Don't tease me, Pepper," he warned in a tone that set my belly on fire.

I closed my lips around his shaft, taking it down to the back of my throat.

"Fuck." He threaded a hand through my curls with a firm grip, holding the crown of my head for support.

From experience, I knew I gave good head, but with Connor, I wanted to try harder. I wanted him to lose himself. I sucked and swirled my tongue back and forth, getting a rhythm that had his breaths coming faster. His hand did little to guide me as I owned him, the control making me soak through my scrap of underwear.

"Fuck, Pepper, I'm going to blow," he said with a moan.

Instead of pulling away, I sucked him harder. I wanted to

taste him, so I stroked him from base to tip and squeezed his balls until his dick quivered. So turned on, I moaned around the head of his cock, then he tensed, his shaft pulsing in my mouth before spilling into me.

"Jesus," he hissed out as I swallowed him down, wiping the edge of my mouth with the back of my hand.

"Who knew?" He gazed down at me with surprise that satisfied me to no end.

Unbuttoning his shirt, he tossed it aside. Athletic and toned, his chest was an exhibition of rippling muscles—*holy fuck*. Was there such a thing as an eight-pack? My hands ached with a need to touch and explore, but I resisted. Instead, I sat back on my heels, admiring his broad shoulders, thick neck, and biceps that could carry you over his shoulder.

I shook my head, hazy from all the alcohol I had consumed tonight and the desire running through me.

"I want to taste you, Pepper."

*Hell, yes.*

He climbed on the bed, and I shuffled back. "Lie down," he ordered, and I didn't hesitate to do as he asked.

"Why are you wearing these?" His finger traced the curve of my hip, stopping just below my belly button. His touch elicited a shiver through my body.

"Let me see your cunt, Pepper." Growing hot and feverish, I watched him lower my red lace thong down my knees and around my ankles. Then I flicked it off in a knee kick, unsure of where it landed. Not that it mattered.

He sat on his knees, admiring me, and I widened for him, unabashed.

The hunkholes had one type—A-list models. Not petite Greek, unshaven women. Not that I was a state forest. A neat black landing strip was my M.O. Personally, I was never into the bald baby thing.

"Hmm," he groaned, and for a moment, I felt exposed, like

he was assessing me. "This is new," he said, circling his index finger toward my sex.

"And?" I said, throwing my leg over the other, closing myself off to him.

He whipped my leg away and lowered his head so he was in *there*.

"And I'm coming into land," he said, and before I could register what was happening, his tongue brushed against my clit, and I throbbed with desire. My knees shot up, and he rested his hand on my stomach, stilling me.

*Holy...*

*fuck.*

Like a propeller, he circled my clit, bringing me to new heights. He thrust his tongue inside me, ruthlessly fucking me, and I arched my back in a spasm of ecstasy.

"Connor," I murmured.

He tipped me over with his tongue inside me and his hand circling my clit. Instead of pulling back, he kept it there while my body convulsed like he couldn't get enough.

*Fuck me. The man had skills.*

And he wasn't stopping. *Oh my.* Selfishly, I didn't want him to stop. I balled my fists at the side of the bed to keep myself from grabbing his head.

My skin scorched with heat. *How could he breathe?* Connor's nose was pressed against my nub while his tongue darted in and out of me. If his hands weren't holding me still, I would have rocked into him, seeking more.

"Your cunt is delicious," he said, pulling out momentarily for air.

I looked down, his eyes dark and dirty. He pulled his tongue back, and I whimpered at the loss, but I was soon moaning as he lapped at my clit while his fingers teased me, in and out. He fucked me with one, then two at a time, increasing the pace.

I couldn't handle the pressure. My body coiled around him, and my thighs tensed. I released my grip on the sheets and reached for his head as he dragged his mouth on my nub, blowing cold air. *Fuck.* Every nerve ending came alive, and I exploded, this time with his name on my lips. My chest rose and fell, my heart about to take flight. *Holy hell.*

Delirious, I closed my eyes, savoring the feeling. The next thing I knew, everything faded to black.

\* \* \*

A headache throbbed between my temples, and I squinted, trying to open my eyes, but the daylight was too bright.

*Where was I?*

After my eyes adjusted, I turned to my left. Connor laid beside me, a sheet loosely draped across his lower half, revealing his bare chest. Chiseled muscles contoured down his front to his delicious V.

Everything about last night came flooding back—his hands on my skin melting the fire he lit between my legs and his tongue inside me made me reach new heights Jake hadn't even attempted.

Guilt should have plagued me, but it really didn't. Knowing Lourde was with Connor's best friend, Barrett, I didn't feel all that guilty. Did that make me a rotten friend? Probably. Would Lourde understand? Most likely, but she didn't need to know. We hadn't technically slept together.

The last thing I recalled was lying sated after two orgasms and closing my eyes with him beside me.

The throbbing in my head was getting worse. I needed to do something, but before I slipped out of bed, I picked up the sheet with a pincer grip, stealing one last peek of his thick and oversized shaft. I tiled my head admiring him and quickly shook away the thought of waking him up with my lips around his girth.

*One night only.*

Buck-naked, I tiptoed around his bed, trying not to wake him as I searched for my clothes. Bunched up beside his armchair was my designer red dress.

My G-string? *Where was it?*

I tiptoed to the opposite side of the bed, eventually spotting it underneath its corner. I tugged the edge, and it sprung free. Then I was on the search for my bra. Not too much further from my panties, I pulled out my bra, well, what was left of it. Torn apart from the front, I giggled out loud. Quickly stifling my laughter with my spare hand when Connor rolled over, I stilled, expecting him to wake up, but he didn't. I searched for the other half but gave up when it wasn't nearby.

The red-hot memory of him ripping it into two and squeezing my tits woke up my lady parts. Hungover as all hell, they wanted to come out and play. I shook my head, trying to push aside the thoughts that raced through my mind.

*No, it was just a one-time thing.*

I bundled up my things and walked out gingerly, closing the door behind me. As soon as it clicked, I slid on my panties and dress, zipping it up as far as I could go before it jammed. Realizing the zipper was broken, I still tried to force it further, but it didn't budge.

*Oh, fuck it.*

My head was like a sledgehammer.

I walked from his bedroom into the living room, and located my Vuitton purse, then took out my phone. *Dammit*—three missed calls from Jake and a message flashed up on the screen.

**Jake**: *Miss you, Pepps.*

Ugh, I hated it when he called me that.

I groaned. My head ached like a bull in a cage, relentlessly pounding at the gates. I tossed my phone in my bag, not wanting to deal with Jake now, and rubbed my temples as I scanned his kitchen.

Surely, Connor would have something for pain relief. It was common knowledge Connor had upped his drinking, so much so that Lourde had voiced her concern to me just recently. He had to have something. I opened cabinet doors in his vast kitchen that stretched the length of the ten-foot marble countertop, trying to locate it. Eventually, I found a tub full of pharmacy products.

Thankfully, the bottles were clearly labeled, so I quickly found the Tylenol and pulled it out before putting the tub away. No matter how quiet I tried to be, each noise echoed in my aching head. Locating a glass, I filled it with orange juice from the refrigerator and popped the cap, unable to stop the cringe that pinched my face from the obnoxious sound. Carefully, I shook two into my hand and threw them in my mouth. After swallowing them down, I drank the rest of my juice, grateful for the reprieve from the dry mouth I had.

Massaging my temples, I willed them to work their numbing magic. While I waited, I needed food. Greasy food. I had two options. Do the walk of shame and sneak out or stay and make us both something. Laying my fingers on the marble counter—a piece of art in its own right—I contemplated my next move.

There was no escaping Connor. Even if I snuck out today, we'd cross paths again. Whether it was with Lourde, a family event like the charity ball next week, or just in the street, we didn't live too far from one another.

Realizing that, I stayed. We were both adults. I was using him to get over Jake and he was, well, he was any day now about to propose to the stunning six-foot Francesca, the socialite daughter of Duke Cavendish and his American wife in an arranged marriage. Maybe he was letting off steam.

We were both adults in need of something last night. But we hadn't actually slept together. Dragging my hand to my lips, I remembered the earth-shattering orgasm he gave me and imagined what it would feel like to have him inside me. I cast aside the regret and instead focused on breakfast.

*Easy.*

Opening the double refrigerator doors, I quickly found bacon and eggs. It wasn't my usual breakfast of sweet pastries and fruit, but that wasn't what I craved now.

A pounding headache demanded a grease feast.

I was busy making breakfast when my phone buzzed, and I groaned out at the distraction, then reached for it on the counter. Turning it over, I sighed in frustration. *Jake, again!*

Last night at the party, he'd messaged me several times, which I ignored. Then he said he was downstairs and wouldn't leave until I came down and spoke to him. Either that, or he'd try and barge his way into the party. Even though I knew that was a lie, his incessant texts eventually wore me down.

Against my better judgment, I'd agreed to meet him, but we just ended up arguing. He begged me to take him back, making promises I knew he couldn't keep. *"All I did was kiss a woman at work a handful of times. It never went further."*

He begged me to take him back, swore all he'd done was kiss a woman at his work a handful of times. He promised me black and blue he hadn't done anything more. Jake could be an asshole, but he wasn't a cheater, unlike his buddy, Hunter. After a while, I was sick of going back and forth and arguing about the basic principles of a relationship being trust. Eventually, I think he felt sorry for me and gave up. He left while I remained out front, trying to comprehend the last year I'd spent with Jake and what I wanted.

After half an hour, I walked back inside Lourde's apartment building with a hazy head and still hadn't come to any conclusion. The doorman opened the entrance door for me, and as I walked into the foyer, well, that's how I wound up here, making breakfast.

"Pepper." I quickly looked up and put down my phone.

Connor strolled toward me, and I couldn't ignore how his sweats clung to his waist as he drew closer. I took in his tanned chest and broad shoulders momentarily before dragging myself up to his line of sight.

"So about last night." He cast his eyes down to the opening of my half-zipped dress. "I think you're missing this." He split into a grin as he held up a piece of my torn bra.

"You owe me a bra." I smirked, hearing the pan sizzle behind me.

*Was I the only one realizing this wasn't as awkward as expected?*

He moved toward the counter, sliding onto the opposite-facing barstool, then his gaze fell to the Tylenol.

I edged it toward him. "Hangovers are a bitch, aren't they?" I said, turning to open the refrigerator. Then, lifting the jug of juice, I poured him a glass.

"Worse than death," he said, taking the glass from my grasp. His thumb brushed my hand, and I ignored the warm sensation spreading up my arm.

He gulped it down in one go, and I watched his Adam's apple bob up and down as he swallowed, and my lady parts said hello.

"Pepper?"

"Yes." I breathed out, feeling hot all of a sudden.

"Do you want to burn my place down?"

"What?"

The smell of smoke woke me up, and I spun around to find smoke billowing from the stovetop.

"Shit... oh my God!" Quickly, I reached for the gas knob, shutting it off. Then, reaching for a hand towel, I flapped it back and forth, trying to disperse the smoke from setting off the smoke alarm. I swear I looked like my own, yiayia.

"Sorry!" I laughed aloud. When the smoke had disappeared, I looked down at our breakfast. "Crispy bacon, anyone?" I sighed. Downright black and crispy with minimal pink left, our bacon was destroyed.

I overheard Connor laugh, and it put me at ease. "I'll eat anything right now. As long as it's food," Connor said. "You seemed to have found your way around with ease," he said with a smirk.

I picked at the best parts of the bacon, cutting off most of the black bits, then added the eggs and dished them onto the two plates beside the stove. "Well, I've been here a few times with Lourde."

"True, but I've not feasted on your cunt before." I whipped my head around, finding him swiping a hand through his blond hair with a grin the size of the Taj Mahal playing on his lips.

"No, that's a first," I said, twisting my lips.

"So a normal person should probably apologize for last night, but I'm not sorry."

I grabbed both plates and put them on the countertop, surprised by his comment.

"I needed to get over Jake, so I'm not sorry either."

"And I needed to let loose after finding out about Lourde and Barrett and everything else..." he trailed off.

"So that's why you looked so distraught when I saw you in the elevator."

"So you knew too?" He laid down his cutlery, and it clanged at the side of the plate. "Fuck me, was I really the last to find out?"

"I'm her best friend, Connor, of course, she told me. If it's any consolation, they are so in love it's the real thing."

"Oh God, I'm going to be sick."

"Stop being melodramatic." The gooey, yellow yolk spilled onto the plate as I sliced my egg in half.

"No, fuck…"

He lurched off the barstool and ran toward the bathroom. Like literally sick.

After a few minutes, he returned, less pale than before.

"Better?" I asked.

After swallowing down a glass of juice, his shoulders slumped. "I just can't get over my sister and Barrett together."

"Is it that hard to believe? We were together last night."

"Pepper, that's different."

He didn't elaborate, nor did I want him to. We were a one-time thing, a fling.

"So what happened with Jake?"

I fanned out a sound from my lips, watching him stab at the concrete bacon, but when it didn't cut, he picked it up, opting to use his fingers.

"Infidelity?"

"No," I scolded. "Not really."

He turned to me, his blue eyes piercing in their gaze. "Not really?"

"Busybody."

"You know it."

"I thought we were fine, but we were arguing more and more. When I wanted things to get more serious, I felt him pushing away. Then I found out he kissed a girl he worked with."

"Just a kiss?" He stared at me disbelievingly.

"Yes. Just a kiss," I stated.

"Uh-huh. And what do you mean more serious? You're only twenty-three. Why the fuck would you want that?"

I shrugged. "Settle down, Fabio. We all know about your playboy status. I guess, for us, it was just the next step after we'd been together a year."

"Bullshit."

"It's the natural flow of relationships after you've been together nearly a year."

"There's nothing natural about monogamy."

"Don't shit on everyone else's parade just because you have an arrangement you can't get out of."

"So you know about Francesca?"

"Of course, I do. Lourde shares everything with me. Plus, I think Manhattan socialites know about the arrangement. Francesca is certainly not quiet about it."

Connor groaned out.

"She's gorgeous," I offered.

"She is."

I ignored the pang of jealousy knocking at my chest. "Then what's the problem?"

"I don't enjoy doing things I've been told to do."

"I'd say then don't, but I know that's not an option."

"Yeah, my parents have had this arrangement in place since I was a child. Alfred and Francesca's father have it all sorted in some legally binding contractual arrangement that will make both families wealthier for generations to come."

"At least you don't have to go through heartache. There must be something good that comes out of an arranged marriage."

He raised an eyebrow. "You see the good in everything, Pepper, and you're very easy to talk to."

"That's not all I'm good at." I winked. *What the hell?* I wasn't drunk, and I was flirting with Connor.

"Oh, honey pot, I know."

We both grinned devilishly at one another.

"You know, maybe we could explore that a little further," he considered, pushing his plate away.

"Explore what exactly?" I tilted my head, anticipation flowing through me.

"Explore the continuation of your lips around my cock."

I let out a strangled laugh. "Connor, we aren't drunk now."

"Very observant, Pepper." His persuasive eyes leveled at me, and I took a sharp intake of breath filling the silence.

"So you get some last-minute booty before your impending engagement, is that it?"

"Freedom before being chained down. Something like that."

"You could have that with anyone."

"I like your company."

His words dazzled me, but I tried to regain focus. "What's in it for me?"

"Jake, who?"

I laughed. Connor had a point. Last night was the first time in a long time I had felt carefree.

"So you think by fucking you, you'll make me forget about Jake? Is that it?"

With a steady gait, he titled his head back and let out a cocky laugh. "Oh, honey, I know I'll fuck him right out of you."

## 3

## CONNOR

I ran my eyes down her body, hungry like a wolf hunting for its next meal.

It didn't matter that I was hungover as fuck. Pepper was a goddess with curves in all the right places, different from the countless thread-thin models I'd bedded before.

She stood, pulling at the hem of her red dress and deep in thought. "If we do this, it has to stop when you ask Francesca to be your wife, or I decide to move on, whichever comes first."

Frowning, I leaned in to reassure her. "Of course, Pepper. Cheating is for weak-ass cowards."

"Anyway, I don't think I'll be moving on with Jake. I think he's done with trying to get me back. I'm quite sure he'll be the first out of both of us to move on."

"And would that make you jealous?"

"No." She blew out an exaggerated breath, and my curiosity peeked.

I folded my arms. "Do you want him back?"

"I don't know... what's with twenty questions? We aren't on *Who Wants to Be a Millionaire.*" Her gaze drifted around the kitchen, not focusing on anything in particular as she toyed with the curls of her hair.

"If you want him back, Pepper, I can help you."

"I want him to suffer as I have. He may have only kissed her, but the betrayal is so much more than that action alone. Maybe he can realize what he's missing out on."

"Well, if he doesn't realize that, the kid's a bigger dickhead than I thought."

Laughter escaped her lips. "Kid? Does that make me one too? You're not that old, daddio!"

"No, sweetheart, but I can be if you want me to be. Daddy can spank that delicious ass of yours anytime."

"Okay, no, I'm not into that!" She snorted out a laugh that made me laugh too.

"While we're talking about what we like, do you like me licking your sweet pussy? Because yours is like a drug to me, one hit is not enough."

"Yes, anytime... please do that." She exhaled loudly like she had held onto her breath for too long.

"Good to know I can please you in the bedroom."

"Don't let it go to your head, rich boy."

"I won't, rich girl."

"Well, do you want more head?" She straightened. But it was the fiery Greek girl in the red dress who I was finding oddly amusing.

"No, definitely *not*," I said in my most serious tone.

She blinked rapidly, her gaze going distant.

"Are you fucking crazy, Pepper?"

She laughed. "Why, thank you, Mr. Diamond. I'll take that as a compliment."

"So you should. And how about the ass?"

"Jesus, Connor, I'd say to buy a girl a drink first, but I guess we're past that."

"You're Greek!"

She glared at me. "And that doesn't make me automatically want it up the ass!"

"Okay. Straight sex then, Pepper."

"I've only done it once," she confessed.

*Oh.*

"And?"

"And we really don't have to discuss it, okay?"

"Okay."

"Okay," she repeated.

"My bedroom, now," I said with a hint of a grin. "I'll race you."

"Don't be ridiculous, Connor," she said, rolling her eyes.

I grabbed her hand and yanked it off the stool, holding my stance, ready to run.

"Jesus, you are serious."

"As taxes. You beat me, I devour your cunt."

She let out a gasp. "And if you win?" she asked, hitching up her red dress.

"Surprise me," I said. "3... 2... 1... *go*," I yelled.

I pushed off and sprinted across the living room toward my bedroom, leaving Pepper behind.

She arrived a few seconds later, slightly flushed. "Looks like you won, Connor," she said, throwing a hand on her hip. "So, what is it you want?"

I leaned in, taking her chin between my fingers. "I'll take to devouring your cunt."

She held my gaze, her breath hitching as she fumbled with the zipper till it relinquished and her dress fell to the ground. Standing in nothing but a red thong, I took a step back, mesmerized by her womanly curves accentuated by her narrow waist.

"But you won."

"Exactly." The corner of my mouth turned upward into a

smirk, and with one quick push, I shoved down my sweats, my engorged dick springing free.

"Well, it looks like we're both winners, then," she grinned, then moved toward the bed.

"Open wide, princess," I ordered.

She crawled further up the bed and widened for me.

"I like this." With my index finger, I traced the neat line of pubic hair, and an invigorating warmth burned in my groin.

I stopped when I reached her clit, circling it painfully slow. Then, I fondled her pillowy tits with my hand, taking her nipple between my fingers and pinching it. She let out a moan, and the sound thickened my already huge cock.

Brushing the opening of her folds with my tongue, I pushed her open with two fingers before my full assault.

"Fuck, Connor." She moaned and writhed beneath me. Then I pinned her down with both hands, pressing them against her stomach.

She bucked and quivered around my tongue, her pussy pulsing at the release.

My dick was harder than a steel rod. I got up, grabbed a condom, and returned to the room.

"Flip over, Athena. I want that delicious ass bouncing on my cock."

She jerked back slightly, then expelled a grin. Pepper got on all fours like a good girl, tilting her head to the side, and purred.

"Athena?"

I stood at the foot of the bed, admiring the curves of her body. Then, tearing open the foil packet, I wrapped myself.

"You're a Greek goddess with that ass."

With her golden ass in view, I kneeled behind her, and she shuffled back, wriggling against my cock.

"The go-to goddess is Aphrodite."

"I'm not everyone," I said, plowing into Pepper's wet and warm folds. Her tightness had my balls aching for more.

"Ahh fuck, Connor, that's for damn sure," she breathed out in a raspy voice.

"Why are you still talking?" I wrapped my hands around her tiny waist, slamming into her again.

"Because I can," she challenged, reaching behind and grabbing my balls and holding them in her hands."

*Well, fuck me.*

I sunk in and out of her harder and faster. Her ass jiggling against me with each impact, round and pert, it was wider than my hips and irre-fucking-sistible. She squeezed my balls tight.

"Fuck, this ass, Pepper, it's edible," I said, slapping it.

She groaned out. Lifting her head and arching her back, she absorbed every punishing thrust I gave her. When she dropped her hand, I knew she was close. A blush climbed her back, and I reached for her tits, squeezing them while fucking her harder.

"Connor, fuck," she said as her cunt quivered.

I lost all track of time, pressure, and obligation as I came, shooting my load in a pent-up release.

* * *

This week, like the one before, had been a motherfucker.

Not only had I ignored Lourde's countless phone calls and texts trying to make amends for fucking my best friend behind my back, but Alfred and I had come to blows again in the office, this time rather publicly.

Running a billionaire-dollar company might be in my blood, but it didn't mean I had to like it.

Alfred had held things against me. He couldn't seem to get past the mistakes I had made earlier on. For example, I accidentally woke up naked on a public street, drunk out of my mind. Or the time I emailed the Board of Directors instead of my mates with words to the effect of "these old fuckers need to go."

Granted, I'd fucked up in my twenties probably more than the next twenty-something heir. But what else do you do with a fuck-ton of money and raging hormones? Their response was expected but, in my opinion, not warranted.

And in my late twenties, Alfred had fired me. It was his way of teaching me a very public lesson.

Humiliation and subservience.

Growing up, Alfred neither had the time of day for me or paid any attention to me, running me like a drill sergeant at a military camp. So now, years later, when he is at the precipice of stepping down, the pressure the last year has built up was like a noose around my neck, tightening like a coil with every day that drew closer. And make no mistake, it was days away.

I rolled over—forgetting about the impending headfuck—and was met with a carpet of black curls splayed out on the pillow as Pepper drew in soft breaths.

It had been a week since Pepper and I had fucked, and after the week from Hell, I'd invited her around last night. Being the weekend, I hadn't cared that she'd stayed over last night. She was a welcome distraction from the work that was never-ending.

This close, I took in her features. She was so unusual looking—petite nose on a wide face, with large features. Lips so thick and soft, you just wanted to sink your teeth into them. Black unruly eyebrows framed her eyes, and the blanket of long eyelashes brushed her rose-colored cheeks.

The piercing ring of a phone cut through my gaze. Startled, she opened her eyes to find me staring.

*Yes, I was creeping.*

She rolled over, exposing her bare back while reaching for her phone on the nightstand.

"Shit, it's Lourde, again," she said in a panicked voice.
"Just take it." I groaned.
"Lourde." She bolted upright, leaning against the leather headboard.
"Hey, Pepper, finally!"
Lourde's voice shrieked down the line loud enough for me to hear.
"Oh, hey," she said in a high-pitched voice.
I nudged Pepper. Even I knew she sounded *off*.
"You all right? Where have you been? I've tried calling."
She scolded me with her dark brown eyes and returned to her conversation.
"Yes, I know, sorry, I just had the flu, so I'm laying low."
"Since when?"
"I think all that boozing at your party hit me over the head the next day."
"Do you need me to come by and make you some soup or something?"
"No!" Pepper yelled, and I could tell she felt uneasy.
"Okay, I know you're stubborn, but geez."
"Thanks, hun, but I'll be fine," she said, smoothing it over.
"Hey, by the way, what happened to you at the party? You just disappeared."
*Oh fuck*. Pepper threw me a startled expression, and I couldn't help but drag my hand up her exposed thigh.
"Oh, did I?"
"Yes, Grace and I were worried."
A nervous laugh escaped Pepper's mouth.
"Did you get lucky, Pepper Little?"
"Okay, fine. Don't ask me his name because I couldn't tell you. I was that drunk." She shrugged, putting her hand against my lips in a pathetic effort to shut me up.
"Oh, hell to Jake then!"
"Jake, who?" Pepper teased out.

"Well, you best get better because next weekend is the ball, and there will be some gorgeous men there."

"Oh, I wouldn't miss the annual ball for anything!" Pepper said, genuinely excited.

"Speaking of the ball, Finigan is going."

"Finigan, the man your mother set you up with a few weeks ago, Finigan?"

*"How many other Finigan's do we know, Pepper?"*

"True. And how do you know he will be there?" Pepper asked in an accusatory tone.

"I bumped into him the other day in Brooklyn."

"Interesting. And how did he react to the news of you and Barrett?"

"He asked if we ever stood a chance."

"Oh, bless him."

"And he said he thinks I'm a rare and special breed."

"That's sweet apart from the animal reference."

"Pepper, come on! It was kind of sweet, actually."

"Wait, do you like him, Lourde?"

*"Of course not. I'm in love with Barrett."*

Oh God, my sister was in love with Barrett. How did we go from me just finding out about them last week to them being in love?

"Uh, huh," Pepper said, taking me in.

*"Oh, and he's in love with me."*

"He said it?" Pepper's eyes widened at my sister's admission while I couldn't believe what I was hearing. This wasn't the Barrett I knew.

*"He said it, Pepper!"* she shouted down the line.

"Oh hun, I'm so happy for you," Pepper said, tossing back a wayward curl on her cheek.

Bored and growing old here, I'd heard enough. I continued further up the inside of Pepper's thigh, brushing my fingers over her clit.

She put her hand over the receiver and gasped. "Hey, I'll call you later, okay?"

"*Pepper?*"

I sank two fingers inside her, feeling her warm wetness around my fingers. "Bye," she mumbled out and quickly hung up, throwing her phone across the bed.

"Holy shit, there is something seriously wrong with you, Connor!" she said, making no effort to remove my fingers. Instead, she shut her eyes, biting down on her bottom lip.

"There *is* something seriously wrong with me… there's no disputing that, Athena."

"Aphrodite," she hissed out on a breath.

"Athena," I growled, my dick thick with a painful erection.

"Fuck, call me anything you like. Just don't stop." She slid back down onto the bed, widening for me. "You got it, sister."

"Connor!"

I chuckled. "Sorry, wrong choice of words."

Shifting down, I buried my head between her thighs and went to work tasting her sweet wetness. She writhed as each stroke of my tongue went deeper inside her. Fuck, she tasted like Christmas. I cupped her ass, dragging her even closer, and she pressed her thighs beside my head, groaning out in whimpering pleasure. That sound made my dick harder, and it only took a few more strokes of her pussy to feel her quiver and convulse around me.

Leaning back on the bed, I pulled out a condom from the drawer and started wrapping myself. When I looked up, I found her moving to climb on top of me. Her curls dangled around her neck, her brown eyes dark and greedy as she slid down on my rock-hard erection.

Her tits bounced up and down as she ground on my cock. Gliding slowly, she teased me, circling my tip to the base. Her insides were warm and stole my breath. She adjusted slightly on my cock when I lifted myself. Then, folding forward, she became too much to take. Unable to resist her, I ravaged her, kissing and tonguing her mouth. Her lips opened for me as I tilted her head back, exposing her neck. I released her mouth, sucking and biting from her neck down to her collarbone to her hard, pink nipples.

Her hands tugged at the roots of my hair as she rotated her hips on me.

I groaned out in a husky voice. "Fuck me hard, Pepper."

And she ground on top of me, her ass bouncing on my thighs each time she slammed onto me. The movement was erotic, and I slapped it hard, causing her to blow out a breath through her clenched teeth.

"More," she breathed out, and I slapped her ass again with a bit more force.

She moaned and came around me, her pussy squeezing me with each pulse of her orgasm. Watching her come was my undoing. I let out a low growl, and my dick quivered, shooting my load.

She leaned forward so her head rested against my shoulder, and her chest rose and fell as we tried to catch our breaths. Tilting my head against hers, her orchid-scented shampoo invaded my nostrils, and my dick twinged in response—a lot more life left in the fucker. So, needless to say, when she hopped off and cleaned herself up, I was slightly disappointed but didn't say anything.

"So, Jake called me again," she remarked like we had just enjoyed a cup of coffee rather than fucking each other's brains out.

I pulled up my sweats and guzzled a bottle of water on the nightstand, my breath finally resuming its normal flow.

"And he keeps mentioning how happy he is," she added, snapping on her lace bra then pulling up her thong.

Strangely, I couldn't take my eyes off her curves, and it was only until she stopped dressing that I realized I hadn't responded. "He called you to tell you that?"

"And some other stuff, but yeah, that was the gist of it."

"And?" I felt like she had more to tell me as if she was leaving something out.

"And I don't know, what do you think?"

"I think he wants you back."

She snatched her dress off the floor. "Fucking games! Why are all men incapable of honesty?"

I held my hands up in surrender. "Don't lug me into your all-men-bashing agenda." She huffed out but didn't say anything. "What are you going to do?" I countered, curious if she wanted him back too, and if so, did that mean I'd have to give her up so soon? I watched her slide the dress up and over her thighs, up her middle and pull her arms through. The glove-like fit pushed up her cleavage. My dick thickened to life like a goddamn Energizer Bunny.

"I don't know," she replied in a low whisper.

My phone rang, interrupting our conversation, and I reached for it. As soon as I saw Alfred's name, I immediately groaned, sending it to voicemail.

This week he'd again brought up my engagement to Francesca, organizing a dinner in the next week between both families. That only meant one thing—it was imminent. My freedom would soon come to an end.

"Let me guess, Alfred?"

"Yes." Frustrated, I ran my fingers through my hair before swiping them over my face.

"Is this about his retirement and your engagement?"

"I'm sure it is. I've been avoiding him all week."

She frowned. "Well, maybe this little thing has run its course anyway," Pepper said, twirling the end of her hair and gazing up at me with mocha-colored eyes.

"Fuck," I said, swiping the entire contents off my side

table. The lamp fell, shattering glass onto the wooden floor, along with my phone and books that were neatly piled below it.

"Connor!" Swiftly Pepper appeared by my side, wrapping her hands around me. She grabbed my arms, pulling them around her waist.

I breathed out a fiery angry breath and settled into her embrace. My dick twinged, springing to life at the scent of her floral body wash. As the tension in my shoulders eased, I pulled her closer, my mind slowed, and my body calmed. Strangely, I was calmer in her arms.

"It will all work out," she said. "I promise."

I dragged my hands down to the curve of her ass, pulling her into my thickness. "I need you, Pepper."

## 4

## PEPPER

Sunday.

I pitied Connor and the predicament he faced.

To the outside world, the Diamonds were one of the wealthiest families in the country. Born into privilege, Connor had it all—model looks included. A lifestyle everyone dreamed of with private jets, homes in Europe and the United Kingdom, tri-story penthouses on Park Avenue, and luxury cars. And if that weren't enough, women, namely celebrities or supermodels, kept his bed warm at night.

But the outside world didn't know about the Diamond family's impending arrangement with the Cavendish. The hidden details with two families that were set in stone decades earlier to make both families wealthier beyond measure, adding royalty to the Diamonds' already exclusive name.

To the outsider, they saw Alfred and Connor as father and son. Smiles, laughter, and photographs portrayed a close-knit family. They had no idea Connor and his father had a strained relationship like they also wouldn't be aware that Lourde barely tolerated her own mother.

But I knew all those little details, being by Lourde's side since we met at school—her family home was my second home. And over the years, I'd witnessed countless arguments between father and son and mother and daughter. Nothing was easy, regardless of how much your family was worth. I should know.

My family privately owned the largest wholesale grocery supply company in the United States. So I, too, bore a responsibility like Connor and Lourde, but at least my parents let me slide under the radar. As long as I didn't appear in the tabloids, I could be the person I wanted to be, marry whomever I chose, and enjoy my privileged and blessed life.

*Did I say my parents were cool?*

Hell, yes, they were, but Richie, my older brother, had a responsibility not dissimilar to Connor. One day he would take over the family business. Richie had what Connor had coming.

*Responsibility.*

Except he wanted it. Connor didn't, or so it seemed. Truth was, in this short time I'd spent with Connor, I didn't know what he despised more, running the company or being told who to marry.

I ended up staying the night again, which was odd, but he needed me. He needed my body to forget and to bury himself in me. We fucked like the end of the world was imminent.

Since I woke first, I watched him sleep. It was nearly midday, and we had fucked till the sun came up, and truth be told, I was a little sore. I'd never had a lover like Connor, and I'd probably have no one quite like him ever. I couldn't get enough of him. But even a busy socialite, I had stuff to do. As I penned him a note and collected my clutch to walk out the door, his doorbell buzzed.

I glanced at the video screen, and a familiar porcelain face stared back at me, freezing me in place.
*Lourde.*
*Shit! What was she doing here?*
"Connor!" I yelled out in a panic.
Quickly, I ran to the bedroom, tossing the quilt off his sleeping body. He startled, bolting upright, taking his hand to his eyes and rubbing them.
"Pepper, what the hell?"
"Your sister's here!"
"Lourde?"
"Yes! She's downstairs!"
I threw a pillow at him, but he caught it and threw it back.
"Okay, relax. I'll get rid of her. Stay in here and don't make a sound."
He raced out of the bedroom, hitting the button on the video intercom.
"Connor, it's me," Lourde's voice rang out.
"Lourde?"
"Yes, who else? Barrett's with me. Can you let us up?"
"Barrett's with you?"
"Yes, now let us up, weirdo."
"It's not a good time, guys."
"Ah, we won't be long, Connor. Now, could you just get over yourself and stop being rude?"
"Fuck, fine."
Pressing the buzzer, he let them up. *Shit!*
"They're coming up?" I said, exasperated.
"Didn't I say to stay in the bedroom?" He stepped toward the elevator.
*Fine.* Quickly, I returned to his room, barely within earshot but out of view.
I heard the ping of the elevator doors, then two or three footsteps. Connor must have cut them off at the elevator.

"What are you doing here?" Connor asked.

"Well, hello to you too, brother."

"Did you just get up?"

"No," Connor said. "I've been working."

"Hey," I heard Barrett's deep voice echo throughout the room and down the hallway, followed by what sounded like a handshake.

"Hello, Barrett." Connor's voice sounded like poison. He'd have to get over his sister's deceit sooner or later.

"What can I do for you both? Like I said, I'm busy."

"Well, that's no way to treat us now," Lourde tsked.

"Said by my sister, who was screwing my best friend behind my back?"

*Damn.*

There was a slight pause then Lourde cleared her throat.

"We were going to tell you, Connor. I'm sorry you found out the way you did, but you will just have to accept we're not going anywhere. I love him, and Barrett loves me. Let's just try to be adults about this."

*Another pause.* God, this could go either way.

"Look, Connor, for what it's worth, I'm sorry. I didn't want you to find out like that. We had no intention of this happening. It just happened."

"Yeah, tell me about it." Connor sighed.

*I couldn't help but think by his sigh that Connor was talking about us. And if so, was he upset we were coming to an end?* My pulse quickened at the thought.

"Where on earth is your housekeeper?"

Lourde's voice was closer now, startling me.

"It's like a trip hazard in here."

"Is everything all right, Connor?" I heard Barrett ask.

"Yes, I'm fine. I'm just busy, and my housekeeper has the flu."

*Good one.*

"So does Pepper. Must be going around," Lourde said

My breath hitched in my throat at the mention of my name.

"Must be. Now I've got a mountain of files to review before tomorrow's board meeting, so I think you guys should leave."

"Leave? We just got here!" Lourde said, ignoring him and making her way into the kitchen. "At least let me have a quick espresso."

"Make it quick. You know where everything is, Lourde," Connor said in a resigned tone.

You couldn't argue with Lourde when she was like that, and only doing so would make Connor appear guilty.

"Well, Jesus, not through this mountain of plates and glassware. It's like you had a party here or something." She clattered around, opening cupboards. "Do you guys want one?"

"Yes," they both said at the same time.

"So, is Alfred busting your balls again?"

"Always."

The sound of the coffee machine cut through their exchange.

"I'm just busy doing board stuff, you know? So tell me, what's happening with you? Any closer to finding out who's after you and determined to ruin you?" Connor asked.

"Getting there. But are we seriously going to talk about this right now, or are we going to address the beef between us?"

"What can I do? You fucked my sister. I can either punch you out or accept it."

"Okay, for starters, you know you couldn't punch me out. I've got at least twenty pounds of muscle on you."

He let out a laugh. "It's not about brawn, and I'd call it ten even."

"I know I'm not what you and your mom wanted for her. I'm not old money. But we're happy. I promise you, she means the goddamn world to me, and I'd do anything to protect her. I love her, Connor. She knows me, she knows everything about me, and she accepts me for who I am. She doesn't want to change me. She loves me. Do you know how rare that is for guys like us?"

*Oh wow.* I doubt Jake would ever speak of me like Barrett had just spoken about Lourde.

The smell of coffee filled the penthouse, and I heard Lourde's heels click against the wooden flooring, presumably to hand over coffees to Connor and her lover.

"You guys are the real deal, aren't you?" Connor questioned.

"I'm all in when it comes to your sister."

"Me too," Lourde said.

*Oh. Emotion overwhelmed me. I was so truly happy that Lourde had found her person.*

A few moments passed, and I couldn't tell what was happening.

"Well then, fuck it, I can't stop you." Connor let out a sigh.

"Are you serious?" Lourde asked. And I had to admit, I, too, was surprised by Connor's complete turnaround.

"Yeah, you're not talking out your ass, are you?" Barrett jested, and I held my hand up to my mouth, stifling a laugh.

"I'm serious. Just don't fuck it up," Connor warned in that dominant tone that did something to my insides.

"I didn't think you'd be this cool." There was a pause and some movement before she added, "Thank you, we've always been close, but this means the world to me."

"Truth be told, I really don't think you would have stayed away from him if I hadn't given you my blessing."

"Probably not," Lourde said.

"It means the world to me that you can find it in your heart to be happy for us, Connor."

An insect flew from outside the window, scaring the bejesus

out of me. I jerked quickly, my hand connecting with the art on his console, sending it flying to the floor.

I held my breath, pulling up more still than a statue.

"What was that?" Lourde asked.

*Oh fuck, fuck, fuck.*

"Nothing. I've just got the window open." Connor's tone was clipped. The sound of footsteps made me jerk back, uncertain if someone was coming.

"Anyway, I'm glad you guys are happy, and we shared this moment. It's been great, but I really have to get back to work. Alfred wants me to present tomorrow being Monday with the board, so I'd really appreciate it if we might organize a lunch this week, or I'll see you at the ball on Saturday."

"Sure thing, buddy," Barrett said.

Footsteps followed and weren't as pronounced as if they were walking away. Hopefully, it meant they were moving toward the elevators.

*Oh, thank God.*

"Is someone here?" Lourde asked.

*Shit!* I held my breath.

"No," Connor asserted as he banged the call button four or five times in quick succession.

"There is, Isn't there?" Lorde asked. "Who is she?"

*Hell no.*

"No one," Connor said.

The doors pinged open.

*Go inside. Please!*

"I'll see you on Saturday. Be good to her," Connor said in his serious tone.

"Always," Barrett said.

"And you be good to whoever is in there." Lourde let out a giggle.

"I'm working now. Would you just go already!" Connor said, with a slight inflection in his tone.

"Bye, brother, love you."

The doors pinged close, and I released the breath I was holding, slightly dizzy from holding it in for so long.

"You can come out now, Pepper… if you dare." His voice had an edge, which I was all too familiar with.

The close call had me on edge, and an insatiable need came over me. A warmth scaled my thighs and swirled in my stomach before pooling between my legs.

"I think you should come in here," I purred out in a low whisper.

## 5

## CONNOR

Tuesday

I woke to the news of my best friend and construction mogul being accused of sexual harassment. Around Diamond headquarters, it was mayhem, and Alfred and the board were in overdrive. Damage control of a century-old reputation had been tarnished overnight, and all because of Lourde's relationship with Barrett Black.

I attempted to call Barrett a few times throughout the day, but he didn't pick up as expected. Neither did Lourde.

If we were in damage control, I imagined Barrett and his team would also be working around the clock to clear his name, hence the silence on his part.

The thing is, anyone who knew Barrett knew he wasn't the type of guy to do anything like what the woman accused him of doing, but that didn't matter. But that didn't put him in the clear. In this day and age, we lived and died by our reputation, and the news had spread like wildfire, syndicated immediately with every online media platform from here to the West Coast. Some of our affiliate companies in the Pacific had also picked up the news, with Australia and New Zealand running the story.

Seeing them together at my place on Sunday made me realize just how much they actually meant to one another. This still completely blew my mind because I never thought Barrett was the type to be tied down. That's why this whole thing was a clusterfuck of epic proportions.

I scanned my emails, finding the email containing the transcript of the morning's emergency crisis meeting. Clicking on the delete button, I huffed out a breath. I didn't need a reminder of the meeting with the board and Alfred this morning.

In the meeting this morning, I recommended to Alfred and the board not to run the story about Barrett. An argument ensued, and of course, after a vote, they took his side. He had his old buddies in his pocket like a rat hole—every one of them. Each of them had a dick and balls that were likely shriveled up in their wives' purses.

But Alfred was always about the bottom line, always about the truth, never one to upset the course of justice. From a business perspective, it made sense, but there were other ways. Different ways he hadn't considered. Where I was more about real old-school investigative journalism, he was all about the clickbait headlines. We couldn't be more different.

As my emails cleared to a barely manageable inbox and the day turned into night, I looked up and noticed he was staring at me. Glaring back, I shot him bullets.

*Fuck!*

My leave-me-the-fuck-alone-glare backfired because now he'd closed his laptop and was walking around his desk commanding his way across the floor and toward my office.

Quickly, I pressed the button on my com to my assistant. "Genevieve, I don't want to be disturbed. By anyone."

"But, sir, Mr. Diamond is on his way," she said, her voice low and muffled.

"I don't care," I said in a caustic tone I usually reserved just for my father.

"Um, okay."

"*Genevieve.*" My father's brittle voice rumbled through the speaker.

The truth was, I wasn't afraid of Alfred. Far from it. I loathed the man that was absent for most of my young life, a time when I needed a father and connection. When he decided to notice me after my tertiary studies at the best schools and colleges, he'd only done so to groom me for his replacement—deciding that any fuck-ups on my part would be treated with the harshest consequences.

I wasn't the best man for the job. I was his son, his blood, so automatically, that made me *the* person.

My door swung open, and Alfred stepped in, followed by a distraught-looking Genevieve.

"I'm so sorry, sir," Genevieve said, blinking uncontrollably, something she did when nervous.

"So much for holding all my calls," I said, and Genevieve's shoulders slumped. Then she stepped back, pulling the door closed behind her.

I didn't need to be such a dick. I knew exactly how persistent my father could be, and nothing Genevieve could have said or done would have prevented him from being in my office. I'd be sure to apologize after this cock leaves me the fuck alone.

He made his way into my office, and I made no move to get up from my seat behind the mahogany desk.

"You've been ignoring me all day, and we have a family

situation, a family crisis. We are meeting for dinner at the house."

"We spoke this morning. We had a crisis meeting where you ignored me completely when I suggested we slow down the syndication of the allegations leveled at Barrett. You and your board buddies laughed, remember? Or at your senile age, has your memory completely been swiped?"

"We cannot alter the news," he said, leaning against the chair.

"That's bullshit, and you know it. A certain story about a woman named Leila vanished from the bulletin years ago, or did you forget about that too?"

His hand flew up in a rage. "Don't you dare mention her name around here, or I'll squash your inheritance so fast you'll be homeless before you even realize what happened."

*Asshole.*

"Fuck you," I spat out.

"Heard that before." He shrugged, feigning indifference.

Rumors of an affair with a woman called Leila had been the talk of tight-knit Manhattan circles for decades, but when the rumors got into the hands of journalists, they suddenly vanished overnight, with all fingers pointing to Alfred.

"What are you really here for, Alfred?"

He made himself right at home, taking a seat on the leather and chrome armchair opposite.

"You know why I'm here."

I slammed my fist down. "No."

"Yes." Calmly and authoritatively, his tone was completely different from his earlier tone.

"We are a family in crisis. Our reputation is in tatters. House at six o'clock tonight. You, me, your sister, and Barrett. She can no longer see Barrett."

"For this to be forgotten and swept under the rug, my

retirement will be announced after the family charity ball next week. Distraction mitigates catastrophe."

Pain lashed my chest as I felt my rib cage tighten. Suddenly, my crisp white collar cut off any breathing room. Sliding my finger between my neck and the fabric on my collar, I tried to create some breathing space.

"We need a good news story. My retirement means your engagement to Francesca can be announced. That was always the deal."

"I don't want to marry Francesca." My hands balled into a fist on my thighs.

"As Diamond men, we don't have other choices. See all this?" He flapped his hands around like his royal highness. Maybe he was channeling his friend the Duke.

"Your granddad and great-great-grandfather before him worked their butts off to build this empire. None of this just happens automatically. The wealth that you've been born into comes with privilege. And yours is to marry Francesca. That way, the Diamond name will marry into royalty and continue to be wealthy and noble for generations to come."

"And how much do they get out of this exactly?"

"Plenty. It's an amicable deal for everyone involved. That is why it was penned decades ago when you were both born, just years apart. Genius if you ask me." He let out a sly smile.

"It's a good thing I didn't ask you, Ein-fucking-stein."

"The announcement will be forthcoming. I've informed the board of my decision to step down in one week."

*Fuck me. This was fast becoming a nightmare.*

My fists tightened, the skin around my knuckles burning.

"They will leak it slowly, filtering today's media, burying the sleuth of articles around Barrett and Lourde."

*Well, at least that was something. Maybe he had thought about Lourde and Barrett after all.*

"I'd do anything to protect this family. You know that."

"You mean, protect the name? You've done nothing to protect me. Instead, you've put me out to burn, shamed me, cast me out for your own benefit."

He laughed, beating his chest. "You still haven't got over that, have you, Connor?" The smug look he gave me did nothing but fuel my anger. "You were naked on Madison Avenue, drunk and high as a kite. What could I do?"

"Make it go away."

"No. You needed to learn a lesson."

*Fuck you.*

"Like when you fired me?"

"Well, evidently, tough talk is what you need. Calling the board old fuck sticks or whatever you called them… what did you think would happen?"

I shook my head.

"At some point, you have to grow up."

"You're fathering me now? When, for thirty-one years, you've either been completely absent or a drill sergeant?"

"Here we go. Sob story," he yawned out.

"Far from it. I realize who and what you are. I'm fine. I have a great life, one which you're about to piss on again by making me president of this company and forcing me to marry someone I don't even know, let alone love!"

"Quiet down." He got up to stand, pushing back the seat. "I suggest you wrap up whomever model it is you're fucking this week because this family cannot and will not tolerate another scandal. Do you hear me?"

"Loud and fucking clear." *You fucking asshole.*

He trudged over to the door and swung it open.

"Well, go ahead and write this into your contract. I'm not living with *her* until we get married."

He stopped mid-stride and turned around, surprise etched on his wrinkled face. "Fine. We have already bought your home. It will be a wedding gift then. The tri-level Penthouse in Central Park Towers."

"Great." I rolled my eyes.

"Keep your dick in your pants, or so help me, God, I will make damn sure you get nothing."

*Great parting words.*

\* \* \*

I couldn't wait to get out of my parents' penthouse fast enough. It reeked of a stale marriage and negativity.

This Barrett-Lourde inquisition was moments away, and although essential to keep the family name intact, I couldn't help but feel sorry for my sister. Had I not been so busy at work, I would have given her fair warning and tried her cell again. But I was seriously hoping Barrett would have given her the heads-up about tonight's dinner.

As my sister sat down, she studied me with caring and naïve eyes. Lourde and I had always been close, having each other's backs at a young age when Alfred was mainly absent and Mother would be at social event after social event. Raised by nannies, Lourde had a better relationship with Alfred than I did. She was always quick to forgive. I wasn't.

Over my tumbler of whiskey, I looked over at Barrett. Rundown and tired from today's charade, he still managed to look respectable as always.

Today's events and accusations would have knocked over a weaker man, but not him. No doubt it has taken a massive toll on him and his business, but he was here. He'd still fronted up to tonight's inquisition. He knew what was coming. He hadn't gotten to his position in life by not reading situations, and he knew the Diamond name was everything.

Lourde scanned over Barrett with concern etched across her porcelain face. We couldn't be more different in our appearance—she took after Alfred with chalk-white skin so translucent you could see her veins. While I took after Mom's side, skin that darkened with a glimmer of the sun's rays, taking on a permanent shade of olive.

"Unfortunately, we are here under terrible circumstances," Alfred's announcement simmered the general chit-chat down to stony silence.

I watched my sister, still partly angry with her for going behind my back.

Lourde had bounced from relationship to relationship, but that wasn't me. I didn't need a partner. But hell, I was enjoying Pepper. It was nice to have a friend amidst the chaos of my life—a friend who knew me completely and wasn't afraid to speak up. Everyone else seemed to dally around my last name. I fucking loved that too, but this was refreshing. Pepper was refreshing.

Alfred cleared his voice, the sound bringing me back to the dilemma in front of me.

"I know you have the best team around you, Barrett, but I would like to offer you our support. If there is anything you need from us, we are here for you."

*I quickly glanced at Alfred. What?*

Barrett's green eyes widened.

"Privately," Mom added quickly. "We are here for you privately."

I shook my head. *And there it goes, like an atomic bomb.*

"What's going on?" Lourde looked at me, her face strained. I threw back more of my whiskey. Unfortunately, there wasn't anything I could say to change the course of tonight.

"Lourde, you can't see Barrett anymore," Alfred said, so straight-faced it felt like a throat-punch, even to me.

I didn't need to look at her to guess Lourde's reaction. It was probably the same as me being told to marry Francesca. My stomach squirmed at the thought.

"What are you talking about?" Lourde stifled a laugh. Didn't she realize that's why she was called here tonight? My poor, naïve sister. But Barrett knew. I read it on his face.

"Barrett, you're a smart guy. You would have seen this coming," I offered, trying to smooth this over as quickly as possible.

The tension swirling through the room and Lourde's reaction had my nerves peeking. Suddenly, I needed nothing more than Pepper and what her body could do for me. I not only needed her body, but I wanted her words, her comfort to make me forget about my fucked-up day and this whole effed-up situation unfolding in front of me.

"Barrett?" Lourde turned toward Barrett. Her wavering voice hit me hard, and the sadness in her eyes quickly changed to anger as Lourde averted her gaze toward me.

"This is bullshit."

"Lourde, language." Mom looked down at her nails, then took a deep, loud inhalation, catching everyone's attention. "Lourde, you know as well as anyone, our name is like the gold standard in this country. Held in the highest regard since Grandpa Alfie built the company. You must know there is no way I can associate us with this mess."

"Well, I don't care. I love Barrett. He loves me. We stand by each other in times of crisis."

"No, darling, I'm sorry. We forbid it," Alfred said matter-of-factly.

*Damn.*

"I'm twenty-three years old. You can't forbid it!" She pushed her chair out. "Barrett, come on."

Alfred stared at me, and I sighed, knowing my place in the family.

"Barrett, do what's right," I cautioned sternly.

Watching Lourde, barely holding it together as she left, was enough. I wanted out. I needed out. Pushing out my chair, I retreated to the den pouring myself a full tumbler of scotch and downing it in one sitting. Then I left without saying goodbye.

Sliding out my phone from my back pocket, I typed as quickly as my fingers would allow.

**Connor:** *I need you.*

What had felt like an eternity but likely was only seconds, my phone lit up.

**Pepper**: *On my way.*

# 6

## PEPPER

I arrived at his apartment, relieved to see him again. He was at the elevator when the doors opened. His blond hair was disheveled like his hand had threaded through his hair countless times. His black shirt was rolled up to his elbows and top buttons undone, revealing his toned and muscular chest.

"You came," he said, eyeballing me up and down and undressing me with his eyes.

"Not yet." I breathed out on a purr, knowing exactly what he needed to hear.

Connor's eyes darkened to ink-black as he reached for my hand and closed the distance between us. He pushed his hand behind my neck and tipped my head up, then leaning down, his lips brushed mine, and I opened for him. Slowly and passionately, he kissed me. His huge hands wrapped around my face, pulling me closer and ravishing me with his patient and gentle touch. Everything tingled from the inside out as my body craved his delicate spine-tingling kiss.

He jerked back, then found my hand and pulled me toward the bedroom. Silently, I followed behind him, my footsteps lighter like I was walking on cloud pillows. As soon as we got inside his bedroom, he pushed me against the wall. His fingers traced the length of my neck, resting around my collarbone. He used his thumb and forefinger to gently squeeze my neck as he thrust his tongue inside my mouth in a desperate kiss. The abrupt change of pace had me gasping for air.

Spreading me apart with his legs, his groin pushed against mine. Then, with his erection digging into my stomach, he pulled back as our chests rose and fell. His predatory eyes were hungry, making me burn all over.

I needn't bother asking questions. I knew Connor had come from dinner with his parents, and I was what he needed.

His hands traced up and underneath my dress. His touch sent every nerve alight with a fire clawing at my skin. He pushed aside the thong, rubbing my clit in a relentless rhythm. Connor's touch was quickly becoming something I craved. It wasn't hard when he seemed to want me like an addict who needed their next hit.

*And God, I craved him.*

His expertise in knowing my body inside and out was erotic. He had a sixth sense, knowing exactly what and when I needed him. He knew which buttons to push and how far to take me, pulling me back ever so slightly before taking me up the mountain until I erupted open for him.

He had me there, the pressure building as he pressed his body to mine. His lips on my collarbone, nipping and biting, sent a shiver through my body as he made his way to the curves of my breast.

He dragged my wetness up to my bundle of nerves.

"You're soaking," he breathed out. Even though I was the one with the impending orgasm, his heavy breaths matched mine.

I groaned. His fingers knew exactly what to do.

"Come for me, Pepper. I need you to come for me." Connor's tone was desperate.

When he nipped at the skin of my neck, the sensation tipped me over. I bit down on his shoulder, unable to take the relentless pleasure, then screamed out his name. When I pulled back from him, I was breathless, our gaze meeting.

*Fuck. My skin burned at the intensity of his stare. Could no-strings-attached sex be this intimate?*

His eyes darkened. "I need you to sink your mouth on me."

Knowing exactly what he needed, I grabbed him firmly by the shoulders and turned him, then gave him a slight shove so his back hit the wall.

I kneeled. My legs were like jelly, welcoming the new position. I unzipped him, freeing his strained erection, and my wetness reached the apex of my thighs as I craved to have him in my mouth.

"Fuck me with your mouth, Pepper."

I groaned, taking his cock. Then, licking the pre-cum, I slid back down his shaft.

He hissed between his teeth. "Christ."

His fingers clawed the crown of my head, guiding me toward him. I took him deeper, alternating between sucking him and swiping his entire girth back and forth. Groaning around his cock, I reached for his balls and took them in my hand. I started with a gentle squeeze, then held them more firmly.

He breathed out a throaty sound that worked me up even more. Relentlessly, I took him deeper, sliding him down my throat. When I couldn't breathe anymore, I released him, punishingly doing it again and again.

"Pepper, I'm going to come." Keeping my lips sealed around his cock, I felt him quiver, then his hot liquid slid down my throat.

"Jesus Christ, do you watch porn? How are you so good at giving head?"

"Practice," I said. "And I'm one of the few girls who actually enjoy it." He raised a brow. "And I seem to want to please you. I want to make your pain go away." It was true. I wasn't sure if it was the fact I've known him basically all my life or a connection I felt, but I wanted to be the one to ease his pain in any way I could.

I gazed up at him. He held his hands in my hair, dragging a loose curl behind my ear that had fallen in my face.

"What makes you think I'm in pain?"

He held out his hand, offering to help me up. Keeping my gaze locked on him, I took his outstretched hand and stood. "Because I know pain when I see it, and it's written in the creases of your eyes, the tightness you hold in your shoulders and neck. Right now, you don't have any of that. I've taken that away."

"I like how you can take that away," he murmured, his blue eyes dressing me down.

"I'm sure you do." I smirked, the edges of my mouth peeling into a smile.

He handed me a blush-colored robe from his wardrobe, and I placed it around my naked body, pulling my arms through the sleeves and wrapping the tie into a neat bow.

"So is this your go-to robe you supply all the women you bed?" I teased, running my hand down the smooth silk.

He pulled on his sweats, remaining bare-chested as he walked out of his room, and I followed.

"Not at all. I asked my housekeeper to get you one, seeing as you never plan to bring many clothes over."

*Oh.*

I watched as he poured us each a glass of wine. His thumb brushed my fingers as he handed me one, sending my pulse to space.

I took a sip, feeling a sudden urge to ask him something I knew wasn't any of my business. "Do you want Francesca?"

"I've had Francesca. Many times. If you're asking me, do I want to marry her? The answer is no, but I should try to make it work."

"You should," I hinted, fiddling with the stem of the glass.

"How's Jake?"

My stomach turned at his name.

"Jake has been pictured with TikTok influencer, Honey Jones, on her feed. So much for wanting me back."

He rolled his eyes. "Seriously?"

Strained laughter left my lips as I took another sip of wine.

"Do you think of him when you're fucking me?"

I nearly spat out my wine, his gaze leveling me. "Of course not! Why…" I gripped the stem of the glass and took a breath, "… do you think of someone when you're inside me?"

"Pepper, I'm thinking about how fucking amazing you feel when I'm inside you."

"Okay." I sucked in a breath, feeling oddly relieved.

"It's weird, though. Jake was all over this Honey Jones social feed like a bad case of syphilis, but he still called me three times this week."

"Saying what?" Connor stared me down, waiting anxiously for me to respond.

I shrugged. "I don't know. I didn't bother picking up his calls. Are you going to tell me what happened tonight?"

He exhaled with a sigh. "Do you really want to know?"

"Of course."

He leaned in. "Really?"

"Why is it so hard to understand that I care about you?" He tipped his head to the side. "Not like that. You know, we're friends, is all I'm saying," I quickly added. Although, I wondered if I was lying to myself just a little.

"With benefits," he added with a smirk. "Fucking amazing benefits."

"Exactly, and you said I'm easy to talk to, so fire away." I sat intently, even placing my glass down on the glass table so he knew he had my undivided attention.

"Alfred's retirement announcement is next week after the charity ball." He shifted, and I noticed the vein in his neck twitch. "The same day, they will announce my engagement to Francesca." His gaze lifted to mine, and a pang of disappointment shot through me. I knew this was a fling, but this coming to an end so soon... *damn.*

"Well, that explains the ferocious sex."

"Ferocious?"

"In a good way," I said, wondering why I needed to reassure him. He had to know he was Zeus in the bedroom.

"Whatever this is, I don't want it to stop. You make me forget about everything in my life, Pepper. You are the calm to my stormy seas."

I swallowed down his velvety words. "But we can't keep fucking once they make the announcement."

"I know." He rubbed the back of his neck, a silence falling between us.

I chewed the inside of my cheek. "Guess that means we should make the most of this week."

"It does," he said, his gaze turning feral. "We're not nearly done for the night."

"I didn't think we were. How do you want me?" I purred on a breath, running my hand down his smooth bare chest, over each ripple of muscle painstakingly slow.

He closed his eyes momentarily and sucked in a breath. *I affected him like he did me.* When his eyes opened, dark-blue magnets stared back at me, tugging at my inside.

He pushed his lips against mine, slowly at first, testing the connection, then when I opened for him, he deepened the kiss, pulling me into his chest.

He released the lock he had over me, his hand dragging down to my front. Standing breathless, I watched him untie the knot in my robe, letting it fall to the floor. He stood admiring me, and my heart pounded in my chest, anticipation flushing through my veins.

"Against the glass, Athena, I want you to watch the world go by while I'm inside you."

I did as he asked, gliding over to the huge pane of glass and feeling his shadow follow close behind me. From here, Central Park glowed, and cars moved like a video game, gliding in and out of traffic.

As soon as his head inched closer to my ear, I shut my eyes, the need building to a whole new level. His mouth traced my spine, and his tongue slipped over each vertebra in sensual kisses. I clenched in response. His touch was like fire on my skin, igniting me in a delicious burn. He stopped when he reached the curves of my ass. Using his fingers to spread me, I was more exposed than ever. His finger brushed the line of my ass, and I groaned out at the feeling of him at my puckered entrance. I pushed back on his finger, giving him permission to do whatever he desired.

Simultaneously, he slid his finger inside my back entrance and into my folds. I gasped at the dual penetration, a dirty fullness engulfing me.

"Fuck, you're soaking." He groaned, and his fingers sunk into me further. In this position, the feeling was delicious. I bit my lips, trying to absorb the sensations of the cold glass on my nipples and his fingers inside me.

"Open wide. I want to taste you like you're my final meal."

Struggling to find breath, I answered his plea and spread wider. His dirty mouth made me every little bit his to own.

In excruciating pleasure, his tongue swiped over my

wetness teasingly, up and down, brushing and whipping it against my clit. I groaned, lowering my pussy to his mouth, selfishly wanting him to stop the foreplay and devour me.

"Connor, please," I begged.

"Impatient, are we?"

"Connor!" I let out with an exhale.

A second later, his tongue had gone deep inside me while his fingers dragged over my ass.

I exhaled, my breath fogging the glass. "Fuck," I screamed out. Prisoner to his relentless assault on my body, I groaned in an explosive orgasm and felt a gush of liquid as I came around his mouth.

*Oh God! Did I...*

He didn't let up, pulling every last contraction of an orgasm from me until I could barely stand upright. His hand slapped my ass, and as I turned, he stood. The evidence of my orgasm glistened on his full lips under the soft lighting.

"That was amazing. Did I... I mean..." I blinked rapidly, suddenly feeling nervous.

Sensing my embarrassment, he grinned devilishly wide. "You taste like heaven on any given Sunday, Pepper."

I twisted my lips into a smile. "That was incredible," I said, lowering my gaze to his steel rod, calling my attention.

Following my gaze, he held his cock in both hands. "I need to be inside you, *now*," he stated with urgency lacing his tone.

"Patience, Connor," I said, mocking him from earlier with a wolfish grin.

I slid my hand down my belly, splaying my fingers, then I slid my index finger between my folds, gathering my moisture. Connor watched me like a hawk as I dipped one, then two fingers inside myself.

"Now there's a sight I'm committing to the memory bank," he said, fisting himself with long slow strokes.

I loved the way he watched me. It empowered me to have

confidence in the bedroom like never before. I dragged my free hand up to the underside of my breast, squeezing my nipple between my fingers while dragging my teeth across my lower lip. I slipped my fingers out of my soaked pussy and reached for his cock.

He groaned in appreciation.

"I want to see your cock glistening with my dripping desire from base to delicious tip," I said.

I clasped my hand over his hard dick, feeling the familiar ache from the unlimited libido I found I had around him.

He released his grip, giving me full access. Starting with the tip, I gently rubbed my index finger up and round, creating a slippery effect as his pre-cum mixed with my essence. Then I slipped my hand down the to the base of his cock, stroking him and relishing in the erotic sensations as my hand slid along the thick vein underneath.

I stroked him up and down as he panted, the curves and ripples of his torso shuttering with each breath.

"Pepper," he hissed out in an impatient breath.

Fuck, it felt empowering to have this hold over him.

Without warning, his hands fell to my hips, his thumbs digging into my skin as he lifted me off the floor and onto his waist. I let out a gasp. His dominance infused a warmth throughout my body that lit every nerve ending. My legs automatically fell around his, my arms circling his neck, where my fingers interlaced at the nape of his neck.

He pressed me against the glass wall, and I shuddered from the chill.

He tilted his head lower. "Are you on the pill?" he growled, his grip on me growing more possessive.

"Yes," I said, wanting nothing more than to feel all of him inside me.

*But how did I know he was clean?*

As if sensing my hesitation, he steadied me, his eyes

piercing and calling my attention. "I test every month, Pepper. I'm clean, and since we've been fucking, it's only been you."

My stomach fluttered, taking me by surprise. And when Connor's lips plunged into mine, it was a connection that took my breath away. With his body pressed against mine, his brawny thick arms holding me in place, his tongue devoured me in a desperate, heart-squeezing kiss that had my heart hammering in my chest and my limbs floating on a cloud.

I pulled him closer, my tits pressed against his rock-hard chest. He shifted slightly, so we aligned, then he pushed his tip in, and I moaned in his mouth as he sunk deeper inside me. Our hips moved together, my ass against the glass as he entered me, his full length taking me to new heights. He gripped me tighter, pulling me close. I pulled away breathlessly, and his mouth scraped along my jaw, snapping me delicately with his teeth. I tilted my head up, exposing the column of my neck. Harder and faster, he pumped into me, our skin slipping against each other.

"Fuck, I feel you, Pepper," he said before taking his lips to my neck in a vicious grasp, sucking the skin in a bruising, delicious pain.

My body tensed, the heat pooling in my core and slashing up my body. The sensation tipped me over. "Fuck," I screamed out, coming in waves around him.

He moaned a loud throaty groan from the back of his throat as he shot his warmth inside me.

Chests rose and fell against each other.

"Fuck, Pepper, you are a spice unto yourself."

# 7
## CONNOR

I sat in the forecast meeting with the board, trying my damnedest to erase the quicksilver imagery of Pepper up against my glass wall, legs splayed wide with me eating her like my favorite gelato.

That was three days ago, and I couldn't get her out of my head since.

She'd been with Lourde. It turns out, after the family inquisition, when my parents declared Lourde and Barrett could no longer see one another, they split up. Or, more precisely, Barrett broke it off with Lourde, leaving my sister in a mess and Pepper to help pick up the pieces.

He'd done the noble thing, breaking it off. Accusations of that magnitude would ruin our family, and any association had to be severed swiftly. But sitting here, watching the lined faces and overweight bellies of each board member, I felt conflicted, if not partly to blame for Barrett's decision.

Part of me wanted Barrett to stand up to my father and tell him to fuck off.

*Why?*

Because I couldn't.

"Mr. Andrews, so with Alfred's retirement announcement next week and his son, Connor, replacing him, your model suggests the company's share price will fall by twenty-two percent, is that correct?"

Gasps sounded around the table as each board member felt a little lighter in their already overweight pockets.

*What did they expect?*

Any announcement of such magnitude where a president of a global company steps down causes some temporary disarray.

"Well, I knew it would fall, but I didn't realize the severity in which it would dip." Alfred lowered the wireframes to the bridge of his nose, casting his rueful stare toward me.

"It will be temporary," I said, picking the lint off my jacket. "I will restore confidence during the press conference."

"It better be." William, one of the oldest board members, looked at his fellow golfing buddies, who all nodded in agreement.

"You might have to hold off buying the Rolls till they shoot back up," I couldn't resist throwing that in.

"Tell my wife that," William lamented, reaching for a Danish from the center of the table.

Fred rounded out a chuckle. "That wife is going to send you broke, Willy, regardless of the share price."

Fred is probably the only guy on the board I'd call an ally. Years ago, when I cast shame over the family with my lewd pictures, he was the one who suggested Alfred keep me on. Then, when all the other board members voted against me, Fred voted to keep me on. Even after the email scandal to the board, he stuck his neck out for me.

God only knows why. Going against the majority wasn't something any of these guys did. They all stuck together like the elite men they were—their wives, Manhattan socialites of the highest echelon.

I smiled, appreciating his kindness amongst the vast sea of sharks.

"Back to business." The conversation shifted, and so did my focus.

I imagined delving between Pepper's thighs, tasting her sweet nectar. It had been too fucking long, and although I had my regulars on speed dial, I'd been ignoring their calls since Pepper. There was a pull to Pepper that was unusually strong, and it took me by surprise, making me want to forget the others before her.

When everyone got to standing, I took it as my cue to get out of my head and do the same.

"It's the end of an era, old man." They all took turns shaking Alfred's hand.

"Things won't be the same here," another board member added, tilting his head slightly in my direction to check I was listening.

*Fuck them all.*

"See you tomorrow at the charity ball, Connor."

"Yes, looking forward to it," I said to my one ally in the entire room of feeding bullnose sharks.

Fred shook my hand, clasping it tightly. "Don't think twice about them," he whispered.

Surprised by his strength, considering his age, I responded, "I don't give a fuck, Fred." My gaze shifted over his shoulder, where Alfred cast an eye over us.

"He's looking, isn't he?" Fred asked.

"Always." I let out a low exhalation.

"Chin up. I feel good things are coming your way."

"Here's hoping." I smiled. Letting go of his hand, I walked outside the boardroom, leaving the overweight cigar-smoking men to measure the size of their little dicks.

*   *   *

I'd missed three calls from Francesca this week, and as I arrived at Club Mojito in Soho, she called again. I texted Pepper to come over tonight, but she was with Lourde *again*. My poor sister hadn't taken my calls this week. Instead, she sought the comfort of Pepper's company. It was selfish of me to interfere, even though there wasn't anything I wanted more than sinking into Pepper and enjoying that smart mouth of hers.

Jamie, the burly security guard, spotted me as I approached and unhooked the red velvet rope, letting me pass, which drew a round of groans from the long line of party-goers waiting to get into Manhattans' most exclusive club.

"Jamie, buy them all a round while they're waiting and put it on my tab."

"Sir?" He looked at me, confused.

Okay, so perhaps it was slightly out of character, but whatever. I was feeling different.

I nodded, walking into the club, the music washing over me and relaxing me. After this week and the impending announcement on Monday, I needed to let off steam, and what better way than with Ari and Magnus.

I walked toward my friends, who were already drinking at our usual table.

"Did you invite Barrett?" Ari asked, shaking my hand.

I took my seat. "No, I think he has enough going on." And I doubted he wanted to speak to me after the dinner we had this week.

"I saw a photo of him hitting a paparazzi, and I heard his accuser is doing a tell-all interview tomorrow."

"Yeah, I heard that too. Lying bitch," Ari spat out.

"Have you spoken to him?" I asked, knowing Ari was the closest to Barrett and would likely take his phone calls.

"Yeah, after the news broke. He's not in a good way."

"About the bitch lying?"

"No, dickhead, about losing Lourde."

I shook my head, unable to rid the lingering guilt that hung over me. No doubt, Lourde would put some blame on me. Finally, a server appeared with our regular order of whiskey, and as I took it, she eyed me. Her heated stare cast over me, but it did nothing for me. I gulped my drink down, the amber liquid sliding down my throat in a comforting, familiar warmth that settled me.

"Did it really have to go down that way with your family?" Magnus asked.

"Are you fucking serious? They accused him of sexual harassment and dating a Diamond woman. There is no other way it could have gone."

I lifted my arm and pointed to my empty tumbler as the server came around. "Another," I said.

"I feel for him," Magnus said, eyeing up the busty server. "And I rarely feel sorry for anyone."

"How's the divorce going?" I asked Magnus, wanting to change the topic as my calm turned back on edge.

"Trying to get it annulled quickly," he said. "But, of course, she wants more."

"You were married for three months? How could she possibly want anything?" Ari questioned.

"Where's the ironclad prenup?" I added.

Magnus rolled his eyes. "Turns out it's not so ironclad."

"But wasn't she the one who fucked around?" I asked.

"Well, yes..." he said in an uncertain tone that made Ari and I glance at one another.

"You couldn't keep your dick in your pants either!" I smirked, realizing why things were not so clear-cut after all.

"In my defense, she fucked the help first. Mine was more of a *fuck you* back."

Ari and I burst out into laughter.

The music reverberated in my chest, and as the night

disappeared into the morning, I watched the gorgeous women around our table. Folding her legs over me was a busty blonde.

My earlier text to Pepper had gone unanswered, and I was growing impatient. I took my phone out again, but there was nothing. I needed her tonight. I needed my release against the curves of her body and the feel of her caramel velvet skin pressed to mine. I closed my eyes, imagining the way she made me feel. The way her body made me forget what my fate was.

"Should we get out of here?" The blonde on my lap wriggled her ass against my groin, thick with thoughts of Pepper on my mind.

With the haze of alcohol and the thought of Pepper lingering on my lips, I found it difficult to make any kind of decision. She dragged her long nails against my forearm, sliding off to stand.

I adjusted myself, and she pulled me upright. "Let's go," she purred in my ear.

Who was I to argue, especially since Pepper had taken to ignoring my text?

We weren't exclusive anyway. *Were we?*


My driver pulled up at the curb. I sat in the front with the blonde in the back. Deciding that chatting with my long-term driver, Haydon, outweighed conversation with…

*Fuck, what was her name?*

I stumbled into the entrance while the annoying click of her heels sounded against the polished floor tiles. The elevator doors closed, and she was on me like a leech in wetlands.

I closed my eyes, imagining it was Pepper and kissed her back with a force only reserved for her.

"And I thought you weren't interested," she said, pulling back slightly and taking in the tent in my pants.

The doors opened, and I blinked—the bright lights forcing me to wake from my haze.

She stepped in and walked around my foyer. "So this is how the other half lives," she said, pulling her dress and wrapping it below her fake tits.

Why did everyone have fake tits in this town? *Pepper didn't.*

*Pepper.* Guilt rendered me still.

"It's not happening, sweetheart," I said, stepping back and pressing the elevator button.

She stopped peeling down her dress. "You're kidding, right?"

But when the elevator came, I held it open. Her confused expression was replaced with anger. Not that her lineless face could convey that.

It was in the haste at which she pulled her dress back on and the quickness in her pace as she brushed past me.

"What a fucking joke!"

"Yeah, that's what they said," I responded under my breath and removed my hand from the door, so they closed, sending her away.

"What the fuck is wrong with me?" I said aloud.

Walking into the bar, I poured myself another drink and slid out my phone, checking it again.

**Pepper:** *Sorry, just saw your messages. Lourde's in a bad way. I can't come around, but I've been craving you all week. Hope you're okay.*

I reread the text—*she'd been craving me all week*. My chest burned with warmth, and I quickly thumbed out a reply.

**Connor:** *Till tomorrow, Athena.*

I'd stripped out of my clothes a moment later, and my erection pressed upright against my torso. Turning the shower lever to hot, I stepped inside, the scorching water dripping down my front. I closed my eyes, imagining her curvaceous body of sin on top of mine, riding me, her hips grinding back and forth.

With my hand on my cock, I was vicious. Ruthless in my

assault on my cock, I dipped my head under the water stream, the searing heat livening all my senses. I shot out my pent-up load with her molten-brown eyes, full breasts, and round ass in the forefront of my mind. But it wasn't enough, not nearly. I needed her here.

I balled my hand into a fist and slammed it against the wall, the tingling shooting up my arm. "Fuck!" I exploded, the sound echoing around the walls of the bathroom. I leaned my head against the cool marble. My haze slowly lifted from the mushroom cloud of whiskey, and I opened my eyes.

With the announcement looming in a few days, I needed her more than ever, and she wasn't here. She wasn't with *me*. My fist met the tiles again, pounding it harder this time as irritation burst through my veins like a roaring fire.

I thought about our furious assaults on one another, taking out our frustrations in a tangle between the sheets. My dick twinged, hardening to life, and I lowered my hand, tracing my girth with my thumb and index finger.

Images of her deep-throating me and her looking up through her long lashes had me hard in an instant. How is it that mere images had me ready so quickly? I stroked myself from base to tip, growling out a hiss under my breath. My stomach clenched and my balls pulled up as I found my release, this time to the single image of her sultry eyes.

*Fuck! Since when has a woman ever had a hold on me like Pepper Little?*

## 8
## PEPPER

Saturday.

The Diamond Charity Ball was the hottest ticket on the social calendar, and if you were lucky enough to get one, you were here. Women wore their best diamonds, shining brighter than a lighthouse beacon as New York's finest wore their prized possessions and designer wares straight from fashion week.

Every year, Lourde's mom, Elizabeth, didn't disappoint, somehow making it bigger and better than the last. Forget ice sculptures, carvings, and caviar from Russia. This year was no exception as we'd been treated to a surprise guest appearance from Kit Jones, an international singer from the band, Four Fingers, flying acrobats above our heads and oxygen drips for those inclined to overdo it on the top-shelf alcohol. Chandeliers hung from the ceiling, and the lighting silhouetted the walls and roof and round tables filled with New York's rich and famous.

## Lost Love

My parents were seated beside the Diamonds, of course. Being friends since we were kids and having nearly as much wealth through my daddy's grocery supply company, they were like my second family.

*Heck, if only they knew what Connor and I were up to.*

But with the ball in full swing, Connor Diamond was on my mind constantly.

*I didn't understand it.*

But it was probably because I hadn't seen him all week and craved his touch like a visit to Van Cleef & Arpels, the way he knew my body, every point, every curve, his fingers did things to my body no one had.

Frustration had been brewing all week, and now I was craving him as much as he wanted me. Except now, he was standing next to Francesca near their table, and I couldn't help but stare like a groupie backstage.

Francesca stood with her hands on his chest, toying with the lapels of his jacket. Straight blonde hair smoothed like an oil slick down her back, while a white and black floor-length gown with a high slit to the thigh had her skirting dangerously close to breaking the very strict dress code.

Connor's tailored black suit gripped his broad shoulders, stretching across his muscular back. I imagined unbuttoning his crisp white shirt and tossing away his thin tie as I stood in nothing but my stilettos, lace suspender belt, and bra.

I blinked, the image evading me, as I watched her lean in and whisper something in his ear. She tilted her head back, and he smiled before saying something back to her. A kaleidoscope of emotions shot through me, settling in a lump in my throat. As though sensing my discomfort, Connor turned, his eyes colliding with mine.

Quickly, I reached for my champagne and nodded, pretending to be involved in Lourde's and Olivia's conversation next to me.

*What the fuck? Was he actually doing this in front of me?*

"You okay?" Lourde stared at me like I had a unicorn on my head.

"Yes, why?" I offered weakly.

"You were just nodding," Olivia added, looking equally perplexed.

I laughed, tilting my champagne. "You know me, one too many, and I'm looser than a pair of granny pants!"

They both split into laughter. *Thank fuck they were off my back.* I don't know if I could've lied to them if they'd kept pressing the issue.

"It's nice to see you laughing," Olivia said, and I agreed, nodding in Lourde's direction.

"Yeah, well, I really don't want to be here." Lourde sighed, staring down at her untouched plate of food.

Her calls to Barrett had remained unanswered, even though he had been cleared of all assault charges. And he wasn't here tonight.

The Diamonds had always put their reputation above all else, and I understood why Barrett wasn't here. Being accused of assault was a cross on Lourde and, therefore, the family. But even with breaking news hours before the charity ball went live, the woman admitting her accusations were a lie and that he was framed, Barrett still hadn't called her.

And apart from the brief laughter a moment ago, Lourde had been sitting reserved and withdrawn.

My gaze shifted from the table and found Connor as he walked across the dance floor and toward our table. His long strides drew the attention of the many socialites in the room. He was sex on a stick, and I longed for his touch.

As he approached, he was stopped multiple times by women who monopolized him. My hands curled around the sides of my chair, gripping onto it until my knuckles stretched. He smiled at them, and I watched the women turn into puddles of mess around him. My stomach churned at the sight of the desperate socialites clawing at each other to get a word in. Unable to watch any longer, my gaze fell upon Francesca as she sat back down at her table beside her parents, the Duke and Lady.

A sullen expression spread across her angular features and her shoulders stiffened as she watched her soon-to-be-fiancé stride across the floor like Manhattan was his playground. But she had nothing to be jealous about. In two days, the world would know about their engagement. I, on the other hand, knew our arrangement was purely carnal, an escape from his work and pressures and for me to forget about Jake. I couldn't help but feel disappointed that things were ending. And just maybe, I was a little envious of Francesca.

Connor appeared behind his sister just as Magnus and Ari dragged me into their debate about the hottest supermodel in history.

"Okay, so it's out of Kate Moss and Gigi Hadid," Magnus said.

"Both gorgeous," I admitted. "I'd go with Cindy Crawford," I said, settling the vote with a pick of my own.

But my focus was elsewhere as I overheard Lourde and her brother discussing Barrett.

"You can't say that," Ari exclaimed.

"Oh, of course," Magnus cooed. "I grew up with pictures of Cindy on my wall."

"I don't care how much he donates. I don't want him here for his money," I overheard Lourde say.

Ari and Magnus continued the merits of each supermodel as my attention waned and shifted back toward Lourde and Connor.

"I know, sis, of course, I know that." Connor threw Lourde a kind smile. "Look, auction time is about to start. Let's just try to enjoy the rest of the night. After all, tonight is all we have.

There is no guarantee for tomorrow." I tilted my head, finding his blue eyes on mine as Lourde lowered her head in her hands.

"I'm not going up there with you tonight, Connor. I just can't," she said.

"Mom will have a fit, Lourde. Are you sure?" Connor said.

"I don't care," she let out tersely.

"Fair enough. Well, I still need someone to help me out up there."

He stared down at me, his gaze momentarily swiping over my breasts wrapped in a red sweetheart-cup dress. "Want to be my sidekick?" Connor asked, raising his eyebrows.

"Are you sure?" I looked from Connor to Lourde.

"Why not?" Lourde shrugged. "Plus, you'll be doing me a heck of a favor."

I stood up, thrusting my chair onto the parquetry floor. "Okay, only if you're sure."

*** 

I was having the time of my life up on stage at Connor's side, who was a natural in front of an audience. Commanding the room's attention, he had them all in the palm of his hand, squeezing every last thousand out of them.

"So that concludes tonight's auction items," Connor said into the microphone before pausing and turning to his left. Alfred walked up on stage, whispering into his son's ear as the audience grew quiet. Everyone watched as Alfred exited the stage, and Connor turned toward me, his eyes wide. I tilted my head and looked at him in confusion as his attention focused on the sharp-set crowd.

"Ladies and Gentlemen, it appears that wasn't the last item up for auction. We have another last-minute item for auction. This item is not in the catalog and is a first for the Diamond charity. Men, get ready to sell some blue chips for this one as I'm sure it will be the most expensive item we've ever had."

The audience gasped in rapture.

"Okay, okay. Settle down. Jimmy, can we go to the live item?" Conner requested.

The large screens on either side of the stage changed from the Diamond Logo to a ring.

*Oh God, tell me he's not proposing to Francesca!*

My stomach lurched, and I gripped the podium for support.

Women in the audience chatted animatedly, no doubt trying to convince their husbands or partners to bid.

Connor read from the paper his father passed to him, but it all felt like a blur.

"The last auction item for the evening is a ten-carat emerald cut flawless diamond. Wow! You heard correct, ten-carat flawless diamond!"

Gasps erupted from the crowd.

"Flawless and impeccably designed, this…" he went on for what felt like fifteen minutes. All I could hear was my heart in my ear pounding as blood passed through it.

"Do I hear an opening bid or offer?"

Bids flew around the room, back and forth, then I spotted Barrett in the crowd, with a woman on his arm.

*What was Barrett doing here?*

Holy shit, I took Lourde in. She had spotted him too.

A woman held his arm. *What the actual fuck?*

As I watched, I realized the woman had the same shaped eyes and coloring as he did. Lourde mentioned he had a sister who lived in Boston, if my memory was correct. Thank fuck. Otherwise, I would have launched off this stage without a second thought and moved on him so fast he wouldn't have a chance to protect his junk.

"Going, going… sold to my dear friend, Barrett Black."

Cheers and raucous applause filled the ballroom. And before I knew what was happening, Barrett had made his way to our table in front of Lourde, bending down on one knee.

*Oh my God.*

Connor slid his hand over mine, hidden from view and the distraction unfolding in front of us. He squeezed it in a soothing display of affection, taking me by surprise.

\* \* \*

Wrapping up our auctioneer duties, Connor and I left the stage, and I rushed toward Lourde and pulled her in for a hug. "Oh my friggin God!"

"There are no words!" Lourde squeezed me back, then pulled back, resting her hands on my shoulders. Her smile beamed like the sun.

"I was worried for a minute there she was going to say no." Barrett wrapped his arms around Lourde's waist. She let go of me and looked up at him adoringly.

"I think I was just in shock," Lourde said, placing her hand on Barrett's cheek.

My skin tingled with warmth, and when I looked beside me, Connor had appeared, his arm brushing mine and giving it rise to hundreds of goosebumps.

"You're not the only one in shock," Connor said, his surprise mirroring mine.

He wrapped his hands around Lourde and squeezed her in for a hug.

"We have so much to plan!" I said, and Connor rolled his eyes.

"I can't wait!" she shrieked out in happiness. "And, it's your turn soon, brother."

Connor let out an audible sigh.

"Where is Francesca anyway? I saw the two of you talking at her parents' table," Lourde inquired.

"Who knows?" Connor laughed nervously, then glanced at me.

Connor stepped forward and shook Barrett's hand. "Well, Barrett, you pulled a fast one over all of us."

"It wasn't intentional," Barrett admitted, and Connor followed through on the handshake with a man-hug.

## 9
## CONNOR

I watched my sister return with Barrett from the dance floor. I was so happy for them. Truly. The whirlwind of events that had shaped tonight had me on the edge of my seat.

When Alfred whispered an engagement ring was next up on the auction card, it threw me completely. But Alfred does that.

Tonight wasn't about me, regardless of how badly my parents wanted me to butter-up Francesca for our impending announcement. No, tonight was about Lourde and Barrett. And as I watched his hand caress her forearm and her wrapped in his arms, I couldn't be happier for Lourde. She'd gone through so much with men, and I was partly to blame.

Together with Mom, we tried to arrange suitable men for her to date. After all, we expected her to marry a partner from a similar background and one who could be mutually beneficial to both families. That's how it was done in the past, including my arrangement.

Francesca was beautiful, the daughter of royalty. As I considered my future, I cast my eyes toward her table. Tall and leggy with perfect silicone tits, Francesca was stunning. However, tonight, when Francesca wanted to fuck, I rejected her, putting myself and the Diamond family in a precarious position.

Last night, I came with my dick in hand and the image of Pepper on my mind. Her black curls, olive skin, and curves that had me begging for more, and I didn't beg. I wanted to take her back to my place again and hear her scream my name in waves of orgasm after orgasm.

I wanted to forget all responsibility.

I wanted to push away my father.

I needed to sink myself inside her.

But that wasn't the reality, and the secret, casual encounters had to stop. In two days, Alfred was announcing his retirement, and the billion-dollar empire would fall squarely on my shoulders. And if I weren't careful, I would fuck it all up. Generations of wealth and reputation would be gone in an instant.

Like the countless women before her, Pepper was just an escape. Yet, she wasn't like them at ll. And if it wasn't her, it was alcohol. There was no denying I'd been abusing that recently. Now, it all had to stop.

I sighed just as Lourde's focus settled on me and smiled back, putting her at ease. She worried too much about me. Sometimes, I wish it was Alfred who worried, but that was a wish that blew off into the wind years earlier.

"You all good?" she asked loud enough over the table so I could hear. Magnus was busy talking with Evelyn, Barrett's sister, while Ari had taken to Olivia—a stunning, take-no-shit blonde who worked with Barrett. But next to me, Pepper sat quietly, falling in and out of conversations around me.

For a moment, I wondered if she'd seen Francesca drape her arms around me earlier.

I wondered if she was jealous.

I wanted her to be jealous.

"He's probably just tired, right, Connor?" Barrett offered.

"That's exactly it. Think I need to sleep for a week."

I watched as Pepper excused herself from the table. Her hips swayed with each step she took, and the fabric of her dress clung to the curves of her ass as she walked toward the ladies' room. My dick twinged in response.

With everyone engrossed in conversation, I pushed out my chair, knowing exactly where I wanted to go.

Walking across the dance floor, I stopped outside the bathroom and leaned against the wall. A moment later, Pepper stepped out, and I grabbed her hand, pulling her around the corner and away from prying eyes.

I pressed her back against the wall and pushed my groin into her silky thighs.

"Connor, what if someone sees us?" She breathed out.

"I don't give a fuck," I said, slamming my lips against hers in a heated kiss.

She groaned and dragged her tongue inside my mouth, wrapping her arms around my neck and pulling me closer. After a moment, I mustered up all my energy just to pull away.

*Fuck.* I was this close to fucking her against the wall at my family's annual ball.

"Here, take this." I handed her the swipe card. "The penthouse. One hour."

She ran her gaze over me suggestively.

"Look at me like that again, Pepper, and I'll take you here, and now, I don't care who's looking."

She opened her mouth, and my gaze was drawn to her lips once again.

*No. Step back, Connor.*

What is it with her? What was she doing to me?

I stepped back, giving her space to peel herself off the wall. She took the card and tucked it into her purse, wiping the cherry-red lipstick off my mouth.

"Thank you. Now go." I slapped her on the ass.

"Connor Diamond, behave." She walked ahead, tossing me a wink over her shoulder.

"Fuck, no."

I waited until Pepper had returned to take my seat. The same discussions flowed around the table, and I was confident no one even noticed we were gone. I pulled my chair underneath the table and closer to Pepper. Then I discreetly slipped my hand down like I was tying my shoelaces, but instead, slid my hand up the inside of her thigh.

When my hand reached her upper thigh, a gasp just audible for me to hear escaped her mouth.

"This is just a prelude," I said in a low voice as I ran my hand up and down her folds over her lace underwear. *She was soaking wet for me.*

Francesca approached the table, stopping just behind Lourde and only a few feet from me. Pepper stilled, but I didn't care that she was here. My fingers massaged her clit, pulling a gasp covered with a cough from her lips.

"Congratulations, Lourde. Barrett." She removed her penetrating gaze from me and returned it to Lourde and Barrett.

"Francesca, thank you!" Lourde gushed, standing to embrace her.

Pepper lowered her hand underneath the table attempting to swat mine away, but when I didn't budge, she quickly gave up.

"Connor, till next week." Francesca smiled seductively.

"Looking forward to it," I said, driving my hand harder against Pepper's clit.

Francesca remained hanging back, most likely wanting me to escort her back to her table. When she realized I wasn't moving, the tips of her ears turned pink, and she huffed out in annoyance, turning and walking away a moment later.

"She is one foxy woman." Magnus tilted his head, following Francesca disappearing into the crowd.

"Magnus, you can't say that about his fiancé," Ari said.

Pepper tensed at Ari's choice of words.

"She's not my fiancé," I said sternly.

"Yet," Ari added.

*Cocksucker.*

Angry, I subtly quickened my pace, rubbing my fingers in a circular motion against her clit. Pepper gripped the champagne flute as I felt her ever so subtly tremble. Her legs squeezed my hand, locking it in place for the briefest of moments before relaxing.

When she released my hand, I used it to adjust myself under the table as Pepper gathered her composure.

"Connor, that was rude," Lourde said, taking the bait like I knew she would.

"Your right, sis, that was pretty rude. I should probably say goodbye to Francesca," I said, excusing myself from the table.

"Enjoy your goodnight *kiss*." Magnus grinned.

"Might get more than a kiss," I said, tossing Magnus a wink. Both Olivia and Evelyn shook their heads in mock disgust.

"Connor, gross!" Lourde let out a groan, and the table erupted into laughter.

Francesca was the perfect ruse. And now I had the perfect reason to escape.

I lowered my mouth to Pepper's ear. "Penthouse *now*."

## 10

## PEPPER

Sunday

I woke up feeling the warmth between my legs, the ache pulling in my belly. I opened my eyes, and his hooded indigo blues stared back at me. A glint of a devious smile tipped the edges of his mouth.

The back of his hand tenderly stroked my shoulder down to my forearm. Tingles shot up my spine at the connection. Then his fingers fumbled with my nipples expertly.

*Was it possible to die from too many orgasms?*

His mouth brushed my earlobe, his warm breath giving rise to hundreds of goosebumps. "I don't want this to end," he whispered in my ear while his hands played my body.

*Me either.*

Delicate kisses nipped at my neck, then started trailing down my collarbone. I arched my back as his burning kisses became more urgent and possessive.

His need was my command, and I rolled over, throwing my leg on top of him.

"That's it, sweetheart," he groaned out, clawing at my waist. "Fuck, I can't get enough of you, Pepper." He squeezed my ass as he let out a sigh.

I widened my legs and sank on the tip of his erection.

"Come tomorrow, there will be no more fucking." I rolled my hips back, taking him deeper.

He hissed through his teeth. "I know. Make it count."

"Oh, I will," I purred as our eyes collided in a burning stare. "You don't have to tell me that."

His hand slapped my ass and let out a hiss. I ground down again, arching my back to take him at a deeper angle.

This could be the last time we ever fucked. I shook away the disappointment overcoming me and the thickness lining my throat.

"What is it?" he said, pulling my hands so my torso dropped and my face was level with his.

"Nothing," I murmured, turning away from his intoxicating eyes before this feeling overtook me.

I continued to ride him, finding my rhythm with ease as my hips angled back and forth. He closed his eyes, his breathing becoming irregular and fast and making me more aroused by the second.

I watched him, his angles, his dark features, the strain he carried. I wanted to take it away so desperately. It disappeared when we were one. His angles softened, and his body relaxed as our bodies melted into one union.

I did what I did best and fucked him hard, knowing that's what he liked and wanting just to make this about the sex. But he had other ideas.

He squeezed my ass between both hands, guiding me to slow down.

Slightly hurt, I slowed to the suggested pace he set. "You don't want this?"

"Fuck, baby, there's nothing more I want, but savoring you one stroke at a time is what I need."

His eyes met mine with an intensity that shot tingles through my body.

"Oh." I breathed, slowing down and feeling every stroke of him. His eyes were on mine, and he opened his mouth in an invitation to kiss him. Leaning down, I brushed my lips against his, and his tongue opened my mouth, slowly massaging mine in a kiss that made the hairs on my arms stand to attention.

Sparks ignited inside me as heat shot through me. Then, with his thick legs underneath me and his gentle but firm grip on my waist, my body tensed all over, and a moment later, I was blinded by stars, quivering around him in intense waves. The waves you have when you're not just fucking. I closed my eyes tight, feeling his release as he let out a groan.

*No.* There will be no feelings for Connor Diamond.

It was the last time fucking, that's all.

I opened my eyes to find him staring, curiosity etched on his thick brow.

"You okay?" he asked.

"Couldn't be better. You?"

He grinned. "Amazing."

Slipping off him, I climbed out of bed and headed toward the bathroom to clean up. Halfway there, I turned around to find him close behind me.

"I'm going to miss that view."

"Yes, you are." I grinned, turning on the shower lever to hot.

"Just not yet," he said, siding up behind me, his hard dick pressing against my back.

"You're insatiable, Connor."

"Tell me you don't love it."

"I can't do that. You're the best lover I've ever had."

"Hands down," he agreed.

And we both paused, staring, as steam billowed around us.

He opened his mouth to speak, but I beat him to it. "Well, I'm sure Francesca will fill that void pretty quickly."

He frowned but said nothing. The well of thickness lined my throat again. *But what did I expect him to say?* Was he going to leave her for me? And that's not what I wanted, was it?

I shook away the thought and slid under the stream of water, letting the steaming water wash away my confusion.

He picked up the loofah and lathered the soap in it. As he slid the loofah across my shoulders and collarbone, down to the sides of my breast, I closed my eyes. He passed the loofah over my nipples, the coarse feeling causing me to suck in a lungful of air.

"Until then… you're mine, Pepper Little."

"I'm yours," I moaned out on a whimper.

\* \* \*

There wasn't anything really to say. I was fumbling, not wanting to leave the hotel room. It seemed Connor was hanging back too. But there was no way around tomorrow, his engagement, or rise to take over the Diamond empire.

I'd lost count of how many times we'd fucked over the course of the night and morning. For him to leave this room meant he would have to commit to his new life starting tomorrow, and for me to walk out the door meant never touching Connor again. Or enjoying his conversation, I had begun to look forward to.

We'd always got along over the years, but he never really paid me much attention being eight years older. When I'd grown into a woman, he noticed me but never strayed over the line until now.

Perhaps it was Lourde and Barrett who helped him cross the line. Maybe not.

"How are you feeling about the press conference tomorrow?" I asked, playing with the straps on my purse.

"Fine. I can smooth over investors' fears with my charm."

"Oh, I bet you can," I said, knowing when it came to the Diamond empire, he was all business.

"What does that mean?" He arched an eyebrow.

"I've heard you at press conferences and media launches over the years."

"Have you now?"

"It's hard to ignore you, Connor." I rolled my eyes. "And the other *announcement*, how are you feeling about that?"

"The announcement will happen, and I will feign my interest."

"Feign?" His choice of words sent a flicker of excitement in my chest.

The timbre tone of my ringtone distracted me. I blinked and cast my eyes down, sliding my phone out of my purse. Jake's name flashed up on the screen, and I gazed up to find Connor staring at the phone.

If he was jealous, he wasn't showing it.

"I think you should take that."

"Should I?" I shrugged, saying nothing more while the tone rang and rang out through the silence.

He was, after all, getting married. So maybe I should give what Jake and I had another chance.

I picked up the phone. "Hi." My gaze settled on Connor's, and he did not attempt to stop staring.

"Hun, you picked up. Thank you. Please don't hang up."

"I'm not, Jake."

"Listen, I need to explain things. Can we meet at the Ivy tomorrow evening for a drink?"

"Sure," I said, not believing the words coming out of my mouth.

I stared at Connor, who remained expressionless.

"Okay, great." Jake sounded more surprised than I. "I'll see you then," he said before the phone went dead.

"Sounds promising," he said.

"I guess so," I replied, void of any emotion. "Well, good luck with everything, Connor," I said while sliding my phone back into my bag.

I stepped forward toward the door, and I felt his presence behind me. When I reached for the handle, he stopped me, his hand circling my hip, making me turn.

"I have an idea."

I turned to face him, hand on my hip.

"I can help you get Jake back."

"What?" I sneered, narrowing my eyes.

"Not that you need help," he backtracked.

"Damn right."

"But what you don't want is the same relationship you had before. Am I right?"

"Correct... how would you know what I want?"

"Please. Every girl wants the same things... orgasms, respect, love, and gifts."

I laughed.

"He was falling short somewhere, and I'm guessing I know where."

I blinked, remembering the time I'd spent with Jake. Sex was amazing. Amazingly average in that I needed to use my vibrator to get off with him. Love? Who knows? I thought we were heading that way, but now I wasn't so sure.

As for presents, he gave me a few, but I could always buy my own.

"Respect."

"How..."

He squeezed my hip and pulled me closer. "How 'bout I help you get the man of your dreams, mold him into what you need him to be, and in return…"

"No," I said flat out. I was not going to be the other woman.

He looked at me, perplexed, then grinned.

"No, I won't be the other woman in your love triangle."

"And in return, you be my ear. My confidant in this surging shit-storm of my life right now."

"You just want to talk to me?"

"Yes, most days, in person or on the phone."

"And you think we'll be able to keep our hands off each other?"

"We have to," he said, releasing his grasp over my hip.

"I owe it to Francesca to try, and you owe it to yourself to try to have the relationship you deserve, Pepper. Because you are special. Jake knows it, and I know it."

I opened my mouth to speak, but words didn't come out.

"And if he's your guy, I want to help in your relationship."

"What makes you think I'd take advice from you about relationships? You're the king of bedding women… you, Barrett, Ari, and Magnus are a force to be reckoned with."

"The hunkholes, right? I heard that's the name you coined." The way he laughed sent a shiver up my spine. "I know women intimately. As for relationships, I learned what not to do by watching Mom and Alfred together."

I knew his parents had been having problems lately. Lourde had mentioned it, but I hadn't known it was that bad.

I contemplated his idea while his gaze remained glued to mine.

Dammit. I hated when he was right. The truth was, I could use his help if I wanted Jake and me to work out. But there was also the other truth, the one I tried to bury—I wasn't ready to part with him yet—his body or his words.

## 11

## CONNOR

I handled the media pack with ease. I answered the questions they fired at me truthfully, giving each of them a thoughtful and honest answer.

What would I bring to the table?

Can you measure up to the success?

What kind of legacy will you leave?

Will we see any drunken pictures of you again?

That last question was an intentional attempt to rattle me. *Nice try, asshole.*

"We all go through a time when we do stupid things. I was young—"

"You weren't that young."

Ignoring his interruption, I continued, squaring my shoulders, "That was a time in my life when I was still discovering myself. A time that was great, actually, but fraught with uncertainty. I can tell you I'm a different man standing in front of you and our investors today. My sole focus is taking the reins from my father and steering this company into the 21$^{st}$ century."

Cheers surrounded the stateroom, and I looked over at my

father, who gave me an approving empty nod. I may be President of Diamond Incorporated now, but that's it. That's all I was to him.

Alfred stood up and motioned toward the podium. He'd already given his little departure speech, so what now? I moved aside, letting him step behind the podium.

"As you can see, the company is in excellent hands. Further to the announcement today, I can also add the news of the impending nuptials of not only my daughter, Lourde, to Barrett Black, which you no doubt know about, but I'm pleased to announce that Connor and Francesca are also engaged."

I turned to find the board members giving them a brief smile. Surely, they knew this couldn't go any better.

Questions came firing, thick and fast. My father stepped back.

But I wasn't going to answer a damn thing.

This was on him.

All I could think about was Pepper's dark line of hair sweeping down to her pink folds, perfectly tight and always wet for me and how we fit like one in the bedroom.

"Connor, are you saying goodbye to the bachelor you've always been?"

My mind flicked to the voice bellowing from the crowd.

"You're not a one-man woman..."

"Why now? Is this all for publicity?"

I smiled, stepped forward to the microphone, and the questions simmered down.

"Thank you all for your congratulations. I can tell you I look forward to being the husband I can be.

"Connor, when are you getting married?"

"Thank you all for coming." I stepped back and walked past Alfred and toward the exit.

The press conference was over, whether they liked it or not.

***

After the press conference, my assistant reminded me of a dinner scheduled at my parents' penthouse with the Cavendish family.

On the elevator up to my parents' penthouse, I checked the company's share price. After today's announcement, they dipped slightly but not at all like the bloodbath the financial modeling predicted. *Take that, Alfred.*

Perhaps I'm precisely what the company needed—fresh eyes and a modern perspective. Maybe now he'd leave me the fuck alone to drive this company forward.

The doors opened, and I spotted Lourde and Barrett, smiles beaming from their faces as they chatted with Mom and Alfred.

"Evening all," I groaned out, then pecked Mom and Lourde on the cheek, followed by handshakes to Barrett and an even quicker handshake to Alfred. I extracted myself as quickly as I could, walking to the bar and helping myself to a full glass of whiskey.

Barrett walked over to me, sensing my displeasing mood. His gaze lowered to the full glass in hand, and he frowned. "How are you doing after today's announcement?"

"Well, I'm here, aren't I?" I shrugged, taking a large gulp.

"Was that because your assistant reminded you of tonight's dinner?"

I huffed out a laugh. "Shit, is it that obvious?"

He slapped me between the shoulder blades. "I know it's difficult being the son of Alfred Diamond, but maybe try to embrace the work instead of hating it."

"I don't hate it. Over the last year, I've actually warmed to it. It's just... he makes it difficult, you know? How would you know? You haven't had a father since you were sixteen." I shook my head. "Sorry... that's not what I meant."

He stared at me but said nothing. I knew losing his parents to a car accident was tough, so I wasn't thinking when I made that comment. In fact, the handful of times we'd spoken about his parents and sister over the last decade or so was usually a slip of the tongue. He was a closed book when it came to them, and I can understand why.

"It's fine. Listen, all I'm saying is, you obviously know how to do the job. The pressure is another thing."

I groaned, taking my whiskey to my lips in a big gulp.

"Pressure can make us crack regardless of our ability."

"You're always so cool."

"I think that comes with getting fed lemons most of my life."

"What, so you've made lemonade?"

"Damn straight, that lemonade is high-grade shit too."

I laughed, the tension I carried in my shoulders disappearing. I hadn't realized how tight they were until they weren't.

"So, Francesca's a beauty… could have done a lot worse there," he said, looking over at her as she entered the room.

Wearing a black fitted dress that covered her completely, she smiled as her blue eyes met mine.

"I guess so." I smiled back at her briefly before returning my attention to Barrett, who looked at me accusingly.

"It wasn't Francesca at your place the other day, was it?"

I laughed. Damn, I thought he'd forgotten about that. Fuck, he had an impeccable memory.

Francesca strutted over, and intentionally I shouldered Barrett into her direction.

He let out a chuckle.

"Connor, or should I say, fiancé?" Her full lips tilted into a sure smile.

I rested my hand on her hip and kissed her cheek, intentionally moving my head to the side when she went for my lips.

"Connor's fine." I released my hand from her bony hip,

feeling like I was disrespecting Pepper by being this close to another woman.

I shook the feeling away. Pepper's body was what I needed, but now I could sink into Francesca. *Maybe…*

Francesca's parents appeared behind their daughter.

"Duke and Duchess Cavendish, so nice to see you both again."

"Call me Dad," he said, shaking my hand. "And Mom!" Duchess Cavendish kissed both my cheeks, and when she pulled back, she was beaming.

*Fuck, no.*

I smiled, uncertain what to say when Barrett cleared his throat. "Sorry, I'm being rude. This is my friend and soon-to-be brother-in-law, Barrett Black."

*And savior.*

"Yes, of course! Your proposal was so romantic, Barrett," the Duchess trilled, a blush blooming on her cheeks.

Gretchen, the housekeeper, appeared in the room, and I was ecstatic at the timely interruption.

"Excuse me, ladies and gentlemen, dinner is served if you would like to follow me into the dining room."

Maybe Barrett was right. I could get a lot worse than Francesca. I watched her sashay her hips in an over-the-top seductive way that pulled my gaze. She was trying very hard to get my attention, and I feared that turning her down at the charity ball had turned her attempts up a notch.

Lourde was busy chatting with Francesca throughout the entrée of lobster thermidor. It appeared they were fond of each other, but then again, Lourde could make friends with an inmate on death row. Even if she didn't like someone, she'd make them feel welcome and at ease. That was our upbringing and the Diamond charm.

By the time dessert had rolled around, Francesca was

growing impatient with me and my ear-splitting avoidance tactics.

"So, should we talk about our living arrangements now the announcement is out?"

"Sure. I'm living on my own. You can have the house they're gifting us."

"What?" She dashed her hand off the table.

"Till we're married," I clarified.

"But what about now?"

"Now, I need to focus on running the Diamond empire. You understand that, don't you, Francesca?"

"I guess." She sighed. "Maybe we can have a brief engagement?"

"We will fit in with Lourde's plans. I don't want to take away from their wedding preparations. Lourde's dreamed of this day forever."

"And so have I!" Francesca let out a huff, scissoring her leg on top of the other.

"Really?"

"Yes, is that so hard to believe?"

"I just thought that because you knew we had an arrangement, the excitement wouldn't be there."

"Like it is for you?" She raised an eyebrow.

"Exactly," I said, taking another sip of my whiskey.

"We're good together," she purred, her hand on my leg discreetly under the table.

I closed my eyes for a minute.

Pepper's eyes stared back at me.

I shook it away.

"Connor? Are you okay?"

"Perfect," I said, struggling with her touch on my thigh.

Gretchen appeared with a tray of diamond rings and brought it around, placing it in front of her. Francesca removed her hand and clapped together in glee. Instantly, I felt at ease knowing her hands weren't touching me.

She let out a yelp. "Momma, look!" Her eyes were as wide as the rocks in front of her.

Mom nodded in my direction, and I mouthed, "Thank you."

*A ring.* Jesus, that definitely made it official.

"Oh, Connor, thank you!" she squealed, trying on one after another.

"Sure."

"What do you think?"

Lourde and Mother had left their seats to get a better look at the millions of dollars shining back from the tray.

"You've outdone yourself, Alfred." The Duke clinked his crystal tumbler together with Alfred's, toasting to the future partnership between two powerful families. "Royalty and media empire… powerful, lasting, and life-changing."

While their charade was going on, I slid my phone out of my pocket. An unread text from Pepper appeared and stirred me.

**Pepper**: *You crushed it today at the press conference… hope all is going well tonight… I met with Jake today.*

Immediately, I thumbed out a reply, eager to know what happened with her ex.

**Connor**: *And he wants you back, right?*

Three dots appeared almost immediately, and I released a breath I didn't know I was holding.

**Pepper**: *Yes.*

*Yes? That's it? Did they kiss? Did they fuck?*

Heat clawed underneath my collar at the thought of Jake's hands on her body.

**Connor**: *Did you fuck him?*

My mouth went dry, staring at the screen as I waited for her to reply.

**Pepper**: *No… and what does that have to do with anything?*
Immediately, my blood pressure simmered back down.
**Connor:** *No sex. You're starting again. You want to make him beg for you.*
**Pepper:** *He might not stay around then…*
**Connor:** *Trust me, he will.*

"Connor? What are you doing?" I looked up to find Francesca staring back at me. Lourde and my mother were firing bullets at me.

"Sorry, work." I slid the phone into my pocket and focused on the tray of rings. "That one," I said, pointing to a random diamond ring that could rival the GDP of a small country.

Francesca stared at where I was pointing, and the attention was instantly off me. "Oh, yes," she exclaimed.

Barrett leaned closer. "Work must be fun with that smile."

A nervous laugh escaped my mouth. Lourde peered up and took me in, narrowing her eyes at me, then at Barrett.

I shrugged, then returned my attention to my bride-to-be. She held up her hand, and the disco ball on her bony manicured fingers sparkled back at me.

"Thank you, Connor!"

"Sure." I checked my watch, wondering how much longer I needed to be here.

"Connor? Lourde?" Francesca asked.

I looked up from my watch.

"I want to meet your friends. You looked so close at the ball the other night."

"Of course!" Lourde acquiesced. "I'll organize a dinner."

"Excellent! Will you invite the two girls from the ball? What are their names?"

"Olivia and Pepper," Lourde said, and something stirred within me hearing Pepper's name.

"Pepper? Like the spice?" Francesca teased, flicking her blonde hair off her shoulder. There was something about the way Pepper's name sounded on her lips that churned up my stomach. I couldn't place it nor comprehend it, but I didn't like Francesca speaking about her at all.

I straightened my posture, stiffening. "Exactly like the spice."

## 12

## PEPPER

I sat across from Jake, finishing the last mouthful of my katsu roll and losing interest in how he stood in on a triple-bypass operation at the hospital he was rotated in.

After spending an hour at a sushi restaurant we used to frequent when we were dating, my interest waned. Possibly, because Jake was talking about anything and everything medical at the hospital he trained at to be a doctor. Or because my thoughts were invaded by another.

Imagining Connor between my thighs with his magical tongue darting inside me and making my skin burn with his touch was way more gripping than medicine. I willed myself to focus on the man in front of me, the man I'd spent a year with before he threw it all away. Surely, that was more important than a fleeting fuck-fest, regardless of how earth-shatteringly compatible Connor and I were between the sheets.

Jake brushed his hair to the side, and I wondered if he wore his blue-checkered shirt because he knew it was my favorite. Running my hands through his hair was second nature when we were together, but tonight, I didn't. And I wasn't inclined to do it again.

"My treat," he said, pulling out his wallet and handing the server his credit card. "Shall we get dessert at the new Turkish place on the corner?"

"Thanks, but not tonight."

He shrugged, then stood and smiled at the server before leading the way out. Surprised and slightly relieved he didn't ask me again, I followed behind him, stopping on the sidewalk to wait for a cab.

He pulled me in, and I placed my hands on his chest, creating space between us. Jake lowered his head and kissed me on the lips, then hovered there. He opened his lips wider, inviting me to reciprocate.

*This doesn't feel right.*

I pulled away, not ready to kiss him back.

Surprise etched on his features. "Okay, I deserve that."

I tucked a wayward curl behind my ear. "I'm not ready for anything like that yet, Jake. I need time. Time for me to rebuild trust."

"You know I didn't sleep with her, angel, and I told you at dinner, Honey Jones was a TikTok influencer admitted to the hospital, and we became friends."

"I don't care about Honey Jones. But you crossed the line when you kissed that nurse. That's enough to break my trust."

He huffed out. "Okay." His hand stroked my cheek, and sincerity bloomed in his blue eyes. But I didn't feel anywhere near the depth of feeling I did when Connor's hooded eyes stared back at me.

Why did I crave the dark, dirty, and taken man and not the man in front of me? I shook away the lingering thought and the heat climbing my chest and neck.

"You okay?" he asked.

I cleared my throat. "Fine, why?"

"You seemed distracted tonight."

"Just thinking about Lourde and Barrett and the wedding."

*Liar.*

"I can't believe those two went behind Connor's back like that!"

I swallowed down the lump in my throat. "He's fine with it… now," I added as an afterthought.

He rolled his eyes. "Yeah, I bet, now."

Awkwardness spread between us like an STD at a frat party. "So… you don't have to wait with me. I can get a cab on my own, you know."

"Oh, I know you can," he mimicked. "I'd like to see you again. I'm not giving up on us, Pepper."

The image of Francesca with her hands on Connor's lapel flashed before my eyes.

I owed it to myself to at least try. "Sure." I smiled weakly.

Hope reflected in his eyes. "Great, I'll text you." He flashed me his boyish smile, then turned around and headed for the subway.

When I fell asleep that night, I wasn't dreaming of my ex but of an engaged man.

\* \* \*

My phone pinged, and I reached for it, noticing Lourde's name flash up on the screen.

"Lourde, hey." Blinking, I slowly adjusted to the light streaming in the crack between the curtains.

"Wakey! Wakey, sleeping beauty."

"Damn, what time is it?" I asked.

"Almost nine!"

"Oh, Jesus."

"Are you sick again?"

"No." I cleared my throat. "I just slept in."

"I'm coming over with Olivia after work… we need a girly night."

"Sounds good. Is Grace coming, or is she still in the Hamptons with Dane?"

Lourde sighed down the receiver. "They're still there, and there's no sign of her coming back anytime soon."

"Well, I don't know about you, but I could do with a girly night," I admitted, awash with confusion about my relationship with Jake and my impure thoughts about Connor.

"Perfect!"

"I'll cook."

"Yes! Can you make pastitsio again?"

"Don't you ever get sick of that?"

"A homemade Greek specialty from my Greek bestie? Hell, no!"

I laughed. It was delicious. It ought to be. I'd cooked it with my mom and yiayia literally a hundred times since I was a little girl.

The morning burned into the late afternoon, and after a slow start, I'd made the pastitsio, bought two dresses at a French boutique on Madison Avenue, and dropped off some of my old clothes at the local charity bin.

Just before the girls arrived, I poured myself a glass of wine and checked my phone, noting there was one unread text from Jake but nothing from Connor. A heaviness replaced the lighter feeling I had seconds earlier.

**Jake:** *I know you're resistant to us. But give me time. I will earn your trust back.*

I sighed, letting the breath leave my body completely. Jake is what I needed to focus on, not Connor. Resolved to do just that, I hit reply. I swallowed down the lump in my throat.

**Pepper:** *Okay, I'll try.*

I can be friends with Connor and focus on my relationship with Jake. He can help me do just that. And I can be Connor's sounding board. We enjoyed each other's company, there wasn't anything wrong or forbidden about that.

We could be friends. And friends we would be.

*  *  *

The red wine slid down the back of my throat like water. I hadn't known I needed it until I needed another, then another. By ten o'clock, I was scooping out the last of yiayia's pastitsio and giggling uncontrollably at a cat's TikTok video Lourde had on her iPhone.

"Ah, I've missed this," I said, holding up my glass. Olivia smiled, clinking her glass with Lourde and me.

"Can't say I've ever really had close girlfriends," Olivia admitted before taking a large gulp of vino.

"How come?" Lourde asked while fingering the last of the sauce in the baking dish, taking it to her mouth.

"I'm working all the time. If I'm not working, I'm thinking about working!"

"Phew." I threw my hand up. "This work thing, honestly, Lourde, why would you do it if you didn't have to? It sounds nasty! I'm just grateful my family is rich because getting out of bed before eight is a genuine struggle."

"Pepper! You sound so spoiled right now!"

"I am! I'm the first to admit it."

Olivia laughed. "Well, hun, if you don't have to work, more power to you."

"It's not like that, though. I've never been interested in anything before. My parents would let me. They're not like Lourde's, who don't think women should work blah blah blah… they support me either way."

"Your parents didn't want you to work, Lourde?" Olivia turned toward Lourde, running her hand through her short blonde bob in disbelief.

"The Diamond women have never worked. So they forbid it. It took Barrett to convince me that I needed to stand up for myself if it was something I really wanted to do. Turns out, it worked."

"Hell, yeah. You and I are invincible together in design."

"Well, I think that's you, Liv." Lourde's cheeks bloomed, reaching the tips of her ears. She was so modest. It was sweet.

"If you are so good at design, why don't you start your own business?" I asked, swallowing the last of my wine.

Olivia looked at Lourde. Had she thought about it?

"Well, I'm loyal to Barrett." Olivia pulled at the edges of her blonde bob.

I raised an eyebrow. "Loyalty is a beautiful thing, but it's not going to make you rich."

"We would never go behind Barrett's back, but I could see how it could be fun," Lourde said, leaning in.

Perhaps they were both thinking about it but never spoke about it.

"The truth is I'd love to do something on my own, but I couldn't do it to him. He's helped me so much throughout my career."

"How old are you?" I asked.

"Pepper!" Lourde cried.

Olivia laughed. "You're even funnier when you're drunk, Pepper."

"I'm not drunk..." I looked around, my focus taking a second to catch up with me. "Okay, maybe a little."

"I'm thirty-two. I've worked for Barrett since he started."

"Botox?" I asked.

"None, actually." Olivia beamed proudly.

Not content with her answer, I continued, "Fillers?"

She laughed again, shaking her head.

"A girl never tells, but I'd tell you. I have had no work. I tried Botox in my twenties, but it wasn't for me, and it was super expensive."

*Lost Love*

"Well, shit, I want your genes," I admitted, hoping I'd look just as fabulous as Olivia when I reached my thirties.

"Oh, please. Olive skin... you have nothing to worry about with those Greek genes."

"Well, maybe..." I grinned, stretching my skin tight.

"There's always facelifts!" Lourde snorted out. "I think Mom's onto her second."

"Shoot me if I ever consider that route!" Olivia blurted out, taking her hand to her forehead.

"Well, I won't, but I could hire someone." I split into a giggle, and Lourde and Olivia laughed.

"How did the dinner go last night with Connor and Francesca?" I asked, wanting to know more. I'd managed not to ask the entire evening, but now, as it was ending, my curiosity got the better of me.

"Which part?"

I curled an eyebrow.

"The dinner or the dessert where Barrett whisked me to my old bedroom and did—"

"La... la... la... la," Olivia sang, sticking her fingers in her ears and blocking out Lourde's sex tales.

Lourde and I laughed in fits of hysterics.

"He is still my boss!" She lowered her hands and feigned a disgusting look.

"Okay!" Lourde put her hands up in defeat. "Francesca's lovely... obviously gorgeous too."

My chest heaved. Of course, she is. She's perfect for Connor. Why would I think the evening would be anything other than perfection?

"She had a tray of diamonds to choose from, and, of course, she picked the biggest, most expensive."

"A tray?" Olivia's mouth fell open. "Oh my God, you guys run in completely different circles than me!"

"Yet you fit in our circle like a glove," I admitted.

"Aww." She air-kissed me from across the table

"See, air kisses… that is so Park Avenue… you belong hands down!" We all giggled in fits of laughter.

"But seriously, she's nice, not nice enough to be my bestie… we definitely don't click like that."

*Good. Great. Awesome. The last thing I'd want is to try and be friends with her.*

"She said last night she wants to organize a dinner with you guys and the hunkholes."

"The who?" Olivia tipped her head to the side.

I smiled. "That's what we call them… Connor, Barrett, Magnus, and Ari. All arrogant with their big swinging dicks and all gorgeous." I felt spots of color fill my cheeks, and I did what I could to will them away.

"Can we not talk about my brother's dick?" Lourde said, poking a finger in her mouth. "But I can tell you Barrett is huge!"

"Or my boss!" Olivia yelled, nudging Lourde in the ribs.

"Sorry, I can't help it!" Lourde put her hands to her mouth, stifling a giggle.

My laughter subsided and gave way to uncertainty. I wasn't sure how I'd feel being across from Francesca, considering that Connor had his fingers inside me underneath the table the last time I saw her.

## 13

## CONNOR

Tuesday

Two days on the job and share market had only dipped slightly. The Board of Directors left me to run the company, and that's exactly what I did. Without my father appearing over my shoulder, it was far more rewarding. Regardless of how Alfred had been in the past, he had retired and now trusted me with the company. With him not breathing down my neck, I was beginning to see my true potential, and ideas flowed like an overspilled dam. It was liberating. There was no excusing the responsibility I had on my shoulders, but somehow, today, that didn't seem to matter.

I took a minute at the end of the day to check my cell and sighed. There, in bold, were three missed calls from Francesca —*my fiancée*. I turned her down for lunch today because I was too busy. But the truth was, I'd make time if it were Pepper who asked.

Because time hadn't erased my incessant thinking about Pepper, the way her mocha-colored eyes looked up at me made me feel something.

I switched off my laptop and rolled back in my chair, taking in the view of Central Park. The burnt orange sun lowered over the park, making the trees double with their black shadows. Normally, the sun setting would create a sense of calm, but I noticed the squeeze pulling between my shoulder blades.

"So, what makes you think you're leaving now?"

I jerked. Alfred's booming voice ricocheted around my office walls.

*What the fuck was he doing here?*

I turned to face the man himself, instantly squaring my shoulders as I stood. "Alfred."

"Are you done with your first day on the job?"

"Can't you just leave me alone for a second?" I bent down and picked up the leather briefcase I'd left at the foot of my desk.

"What makes you think I'd just hand this baby over that quickly?"

A sudden coldness swept my bones. "What do you mean? The paperwork's done. I'm the president."

"In name, but I'm not leaving. I may have stepped down and given you the reins, but I'm going to be here. Not every day. Not every second day, but I'll be in the hallways, watching your every move."

"What the hell are you talking about? I'm here. I'm doing what you want!" I shouted as exasperation clawed at my collar like a knife.

"Diamond Incorporated is an empire built over the last eighty years. I owe it to Alfred Senior to ensure its ongoing success. Personally, I don't think you have this. I don't think you have it at all."

## Lost Love

"I've proven to you enough over the years. I've got this! What the fuck was my Ivy League education for and the last fifteen years of my life working here?"

"We need to leave a legacy."

*I couldn't believe what I was hearing.*

I let go of my briefcase, and it landed with a thud against the floor. "Did you even want to give me this company, or were you just passing the baton, keeping tradition because you're a Diamond?"

"Ha! Don't you think I tried for an alternative? I even tried to get your mother pregnant again when I knew your heart wasn't in it."

"Maybe if you kept your dick in your pants, you could have... I could have had a brother. You could've had your wish for a son who made you proud."

His eyes bulged from his weathered face. "What did you say?"

"Oh yeah, I know. I know all about *her*. The picture you keep in your wallet is just the start."

"How could you know?" he remarked in a deadly whisper. "You know nothing!" he yelled. Lunging forward, he pushed the stack of papers off my desk, sending them flying to the floor. When my assistant looked inside the glass window, a look of concern shadowed her face. I nodded, reassuring her everything was fine.

"Yes, Alfred, I know about her. Leave me the fuck alone if you want me to run this company."

He clutched at his chest as his face flushed with anger.

*It surprised me how angry he was getting at the mere mention of it.*

I walked out, leaving him alone in my office.

My perfect day wasn't so perfect.

*For a man that made it his business to know everything, had he no idea I knew about the affair?* I have known since the age of six when I found a picture of a pretty woman who wasn't Mom in his wallet. So what else was I supposed to do but run and tell my mom? Except when I did, her reaction was completely different from mine. She wasn't at all shocked. Instead, asking me to forget about what I'd seen. But I couldn't. It only clicked a few years later when I grew hair on my balls, that Alfred was having an affair, and what he and Mom had was purely a marriage of convenience.

Exactly what they planned for me.

The elevator door shut behind me, and I slipped out my phone, needing to hear her voice.

"Hey!" Her voice lifted me, melodic and calm.

"Pepper, can you come over?"

"I'll be right there."

*** 

My driver dropped me in front of my home on Park Avenue. I walked up, and Emilio held open the door.

"Good evening, Mr. Diamond."

"Emilio." I gave a curt nod and brushed past him, unwilling to engage in our normal conversation tonight.

Trudging into the elevator, I banged my fist on the penthouse button. Then I dropped my briefcase to loosen my collar, unbuttoning the first two buttons so I could breathe more easily.

After I walked inside my apartment, I roamed around in vacant movement, arriving at the stainless-steel refrigerator. I stared at the fully-stocked meals my housekeeper had prepared, but I wasn't hungry.

No, I was seething mad.

*Fuck him, fuck him to hell.* The unwarranted asshole who just didn't trust me enough to run his company.

The intercom buzzed, and I knew it was her. I took a deep breath and walked over, pressing the button.

"Yes."

"Sir, I have Ms. Pepper Little here to see you."

"Send her up."

I paced toward the elevator, counting down the seconds until I'd see her. As soon as the doors opened, I exhaled, finally able to breathe.

Wearing wooden platform heels, a flowy skirt to the thighs, and a long-sleeve shirt that was unbuttoned, the edges of her lace bra peeked through. Her curls dusted her shoulders, and she looked bare-faced and naturally beautiful, her olive skin glowing.

*Fuck.*

I wanted her to fuck my troubles away.

"What's wrong?" She stepped out of the elevator, taking me in. She probably wondered why I was so fucked up.

I stepped forward and held her close. Her floral-scented body wash invaded my senses, testing my self-restraint. My mouth hovered over her jaw, dangerously close to her lips. Like a magnet, she pulled me in, my body screaming with need. It took the pull of the earth to tilt my head and kiss her on the cheek. Reluctantly.

*I wondered if she felt the hitch in my breath.*

She stepped away, creating space between us.

"T-tell me what happened," she stammered, walking past me through the hallway and to the sofa, sitting in the armchair. *Good move.* The further we were from each other physically, the less tempted I'd be.

I sat across from her, trying not to stare at her open shirt. "It's Alfred."

She rolled her eyes. "Obviously… what happened?"

"The fuckwit appeared in my office as I was leaving today."

"What was he doing at the Diamond headquarters?"

"He's retired in name only."

She leaned in, her brows furrowed with confusion. "What does that mean?"

"It means he, along with his board members, will still breathe down my neck."

"Doesn't he want to step away? I thought that was the entire point of retirement."

"Obviously, not in his case. He doesn't think I can do the job, so he is going to be the machete in my back, watching my every move, just waiting for me to fuck up."

"Connor, I'm sorry," she said, putting her hand out on mine, her touch soothing. I stared down at her hand, at which point she promptly removed it.

"Are you concerned about your abilities to perform the role of CEO at Diamond enterprises?"

My gaze met hers. It was a question I'd often asked myself but hadn't come up with an answer.

"I doubt myself because he has always corrected everything I've done."

"But hasn't he done that to make you better?"

"What?" I expelled the air, squeezing my ribs tight.

"Over the years, has he only pulled you up on things that needed improving? Or is he just meddling with you, making you second-guess everything?"

I scanned back to the moments in my life when Alfred had really fucked with me. Both times I had fucked up enormously. The email scandal to the Board of Directors and the bender where I woke up naked on a Manhattan street, embarrassing the Diamond name.

She looked at me, and her face softened. "Have you thought maybe he is doing this to make you the best person you can be?"

"By being a dick?" I took her in. Her eyes widened. "Sorry." I shook my head.

"All I'm saying is… because of your father's actions, have you excelled in your position?"

"I am who I am because my father ran me like he was in the military. I get that. I do. But why now? I'm thirty-fucking-one. Leave me the fuck alone and let me run the company."

She shrugged. "Maybe he has nothing better to do, or maybe he's so unhappy at home that he can't be away from work."

"Well, that part is true," I admitted. "My parents have never been a good match, but I don't have to tell you that."

"They always struck me as an odd couple," she said.

"That's because it was all arranged. Two powerful families, the Diamonds and the Carsenas, publishing meets politics. It's a wet dream."

"Lourde said nothing growing up."

"That's because she likes to believe in fairy tales and happy-ever-afters."

"Well, she got hers…"

Pepper tilted her head, her gaze lowering to the floor.

"I'm being rude… I haven't even offered you anything."

She waved me away. "I'm fine."

"Have you had dinner? I can order in—"

"Do you think that's a good idea?" she interrupted as she twisted the ends of her curls.

Her gaze met mine, and the current in the room changed so much so it could spark a dormant fire.

I felt my Adam's apple bob up and down in my throat. "Probably not," I admitted, breaking the silence that stretched between us.

"You've got to eat," I said, looking her up and down, wondering what lingerie she had on underneath that skirt.

"Connor!"

"Food! You have to eat food," I said in a stern, nonsexual tone that was hopefully enough to make her stay.

"I do."

"Good." I jumped up and grabbed my cell off the kitchen counter. "Nobu good for you?"

"Perfect," she said, fidgeting with the hem of her skirt.

"Yes, Frankie, I'll have the usual, plus a tuna tataki, lobster salad, and field greens."

I hung up, fetched two glasses and my favorite bottle of pinot, feeling the weight of her stare on me.

In under twenty minutes, the food had arrived, and I was helping her open the food containers and dish them onto my fine chinaware for eating.

I watched her place a healthy mouthful of noodles in her mouth, licking the edges of her mouth from the remnants.

"Stop looking at me, Connor. You're spoken for."

"Sorry. It's hard to forget that tongue and the magic you can do with it."

She picked up the napkin and threw it at me. "Try," she said, glaring at me.

I get it. She didn't want to be the other woman, and I didn't want her to be either.

It should be Francesca I was sharing a meal with, not Pepper. But I didn't want to divulge this to Francesca.

"How did it go with Jake?"

She breathed in, and I watched her chest rise and fall.

"Well, it's a work in progress."

"Tell me everything," I said, wanting to know what transpired between them and how I could help her not fall into the same trap again with him.

"Well, he took me out and tried to kiss me."

My hands balled into a fist under the table. But I had no claim on Pepper.

"And," I bit out.

"And I said it was too soon."

"Good girl."

She traced her lower lip with her teeth. "But I need to decide if Jake is what I want going forward because I know if I take him back, he'll want it all."

"What do you mean?"

"Jake's never been a guy that's half in. He's talked about marrying me before. Then he broke my trust."

"You're too young to marry!" I blurted out, causing her to look up at me wide-eyed.

"Your sister's the same age, and she is engaged."

"Hang on. You can't be seriously thinking about marrying him? He went behind your back and slept with another woman."

"He didn't sleep with her."

"He may as well have. Didn't he do everything else?"

"It was just a kiss," she mumbled.

"I'm sorry," I said, aware she was getting upset. I wanted her to be happy. I promised her I would help her, so I'd do just that as much as it pained me to see her with another man.

"Listen, I'm sorry. I promised I'd help you."

"That's okay. This is weird… you… me… friends."

"I know, it's very difficult for me to stop myself from climbing over this table and pressing my lips against yours, Pepper, but that makes everything complicated."

She gave me a heated stare before blinking and shaking her head. "It's what can't happen, Connor. And you can't look at me like you want to fuck me at any given moment."

"That goes for you too. If you bat those lashes at me again, I'm not going to have the restraint to hold myself back."

"Oh God, we're a bunch of nymphos," she said, and we both laughed.

*Shit.* "Well, don't come around wearing a short skirt… that might help."

"Okay, deal." She extended her hand, and I took it in mine, ignoring the buzz up my spine.

"With Jake, wear the skirt, but don't let him near you. Keep him wanting you, but keep him at a distance. Guys can't handle that... they just want you more."

"And kissing?"

I sucked in a breath, my gaze drifting down to her luscious, full lips. "That's up to you, but don't kiss him in front of me. Because I don't know what I'll do."

"And you think I enjoy watching Francesca all over you?"

"Fair point."

"It's something we have to get used to, I guess," she admitted, her gaze lifting to meet mine.

When I said nothing, she poked at her food. "Anyway, it's not like we'll be hanging out just the four of us!"

"Definition of torture."

"Agreed," she said, and I was happy that she found this situation difficult too.

She pushed aside the rest of her food as we continued talking about Lourde and Barrett's upcoming nuptials—choosing to discuss a non-controversial topic like Jake and Francesca.

She shifted to stand, and her skirt inched higher on her thighs. My dick twitched in my pants.

"You can't wear that around me unless you want me to lift it and fuck you hard," I grumbled.

"Connor! Go. Call Francesca and fuck her."

I groaned outwardly. There wasn't anything that Francesca would want more than my cock in her mouth. Maybe she was right. I needed a release, and soon.

She stood looking at me expectantly. "Is that what you want?"

"What I want is irrelevant, Connor. It doesn't change the situation. And I'm never *ever* going to be the other woman."

"You could *never* be the other woman, Pepper."

# Lost Love

She paused before retreating to find her bag on the sofa. "Thanks for dinner."

I got up and walked her toward the elevator. "Thanks for listening, Pepper."

"That's what I'm here for," she said, slowing down, so we kept in step.

She pressed the elevator button and turned to face me.

"Well, bye."

She kissed me on the cheek. I pulled her close, wrapping my arms around her hips, my thumbs pressing dangerously close to the apex of her butt. She pressed into me, and her breasts were like pillows against my chest. I closed my eyes momentarily, feeling her soft skin and absorbing her embrace and floral body wash. The sound of the elevator made her jerk, and I quickly dropped my hands from her hips, then she stepped into the elevator.

"Goodbye, Connor." She glared up at me, her gaze steely and resolute.

When she left, I took a cold shower and pumped my dick hard with her curvy ass on my mind. The release wasn't nearly enough, and as my mind drifted again to her luscious hips and pillowy tits, I became harder than Everest, pumping my dick again for another release.

14

## PEPPER

I finished the last of my red wine and placed the glass in my kitchen sink, then I leaned against my shaker kitchen cupboards and stared at my apartment. Nerves about tonight were still there, and one glass of wine did little to change that. I stared at my tan leather couch, wanting more than anything to curl up on that with my mohair blanket and watch romantic movies on the screen tonight. But I'd committed to dinner.

Dinner with Connor and Francesca.

*What the fuck was I thinking?*

I saw Connor two days ago, but it felt like an eternity since he'd touched me and made me come alive, bursting at the seams. I still craved his touch. I doubted that would ever change. But it had to.

Even when I had met up with Jake again yesterday, my mind was on Connor and his blistering hands. I berated myself for thinking of an engaged man. That wasn't me. I wasn't like that, but still, my mind had other ideas—often wondering about his six-pack of ripped muscles or his tall, strong, and dominant stature. With things just picking up where Jake and I left off, I should be hell-bent on fixing our relationship, not just dipping one foot in, in a half-assed attempt.

However, now, I was doing the unthinkable, meeting up with Connor and Francesca. At her request, she wanted to meet Connor's friends and the group. Which included me, Lourde, Olivia, and Grace, but seeing she was still lip-locked in the Hamptons with Dane, that left her out. I'm guessing the hunkholes made up the men, with Barrett accompanying Lourde and Magnus and Ari, two of Connor's best friends.

The nude dress I chose clung to my tiny waist and shapely hips, showing off my pert, round ass. Was I trying to razzle him? Maybe. Maybe not, but it never hurt to look your best, especially in front of a man you've been intimate with.

Combing on the mascara, I elongated my already lengthy black lashes then applied a smear of red on my lips. Exhaling, I admired myself in the mirror.

I had the choice to bring Jake, and I chose not to. This would be hard enough, and trying to play a couple with Jake would probably be too much.

My buzzer rang, letting me know my driver was there. I quickly gave myself one last glance in the mirror, lifted my best assets in place, and grabbed my clutch, darting out the door.

* * *

Tables filled with patrons laughing and eating filled the dimly lit restaurant. I followed the host toward the back, past the tables where the private table had been booked. I was late. What was my excuse? I didn't want to endure Francesca over Connor and Connor touching her.

The server lifted the draped curtain to the side, and conversations stopped while a familiar face turned. "Hi," I breathed out in a breathy voice.

My gaze landed on Connor last, and his eyes flared, causing my heart to leap into my throat.

"You made it!" Lourde said, and my gaze drifted toward her. She walked over and gave me an enormous hug. I wrapped my arms around her and pulled her in, thankful for the distraction.

I smiled, my Oscar-worthy performance now on display. "Sorry, I'm late," I said, noticing they'd already gotten through the starters.

I went around the table, saying my hellos to Ari and Magnus, who not so subtly copped a feel of my ass. When it came to Francesca, she turned and greeted me with a huge smile.

"So nice to meet you, Pepper," she said, leaning in to kiss my cheek but instead kissing the air so as not to mess up her perfect makeup.

"Yes, you too. And congratulations to you both!" I said, putting on a fake smile.

She sat back down, cueing for Connor to stand. My skin heated, and my heart thrashed in my rib cage as he approached me.

"Thank you, Pepper," Connor said, his hand wrapping around my waist like velvet, his skin sending my skin alight with tiny tendrils of sparks.

His lips brushed my cheek, lingering for a moment longer than usual. I prayed no one noticed, and as I leaned back, I met his eyes for the second time. There was tenderness behind his dark blue eyes and a question. So I smiled, reassuring him I was fine in a silent message that was just for him.

I took my seat at the other end next to Olivia and away from Francesca and Connor.

"That is a smoking hot dress." Olivia ran her hand along the shoulder of my dress. "What is that… silk?"

*Lost Love*

Before I could answer, Ari interjected. "Silk, indeed, only the best type. I'd say from Russia?"

"I don't have a clue," I admitted.

"How would you know that?" Olivia asked.

"Ari's family are the Goldsmiths."

"As in Farrah Goldsmith haute couture?" Olivia inquired.

Ari nodded, brushing his hair to the side. "She's my grandmama."

"My grandmama was a house cleaner out of Georgia." Olivia laughed.

She wasn't from our world, but it seemed like she belonged from the get-go. It was moments like these that reminded me she came from humble beginnings and not spoon-fed gold bullions for breakfast like the rest of us in this room, Barrett excluded.

"I'd like to meet her one day." Ari smiled at Olivia, and I wondered if I'd missed something.

"Stop being kind. You wouldn't venture past state lines." Olivia scoffed.

He laughed. "Damn straight."

I picked at the green salad on my plate, then noticed the wine that had been poured in front of me. I lifted the glass to my lips, my gaze drifting to Connor.

He was debating with Magnus on which player deserved to get MVP this season. Francesca appeared less interested with one arm draped over Connor's shoulder as she admired her manicure. At this angle, her huge diamond ring shined like a beacon at sea, and I couldn't help but feel a pain in the pit of my stomach.

Something funny was said, and Francesca laughed, pulling him close for a kiss. Immediately, I wondered if Connor had slept with her. By all accounts, of course, he had. We weren't sleeping together anymore, so he was getting his release somewhere else. His fiancée, obviously.

His gaze instantly fell on mine, and I quickly diverted my attention back to Olivia and Ari, who were arguing about something. Words like sweatshops and unskilled labor were flung around, then Olivia started to raise her voice, while Ari had a smirk on his face.

I gulped down my wine and attempted to be Switzerland between the two firecrackers beside me. "Can you two just settle down?"

"How can I?"

"Mr. Spoiled Rich Kid over here is basically ragging about cheap labor!"

"You're not, Ari, are you?" I looked at him incredulously. His movie-star smile reached his mocha-colored eyes. He was toying with her and enjoying it by the looks of him.

"I wouldn't say bragging... I'm just stating the obvious. It happens in the world today. Manufacturing, once affordable in the States, has now gone offshore. We are just another company who chose profits over—"

"Over details and luxury and patriotism," Olivia added. "Plus, what would you know? You don't even work in the business? Your voice might be worth something should you actually choose to work in the family business and not just spend it."

Ari stared at her, venom in his eyes. *Shit!* She'd hit some kind of nerve there.

Connor's gaze drifted to mine, and I swallowed down hard. Pushing him aside, I extended my arms, literally placing them on Olivia's and Ari's forearms.

"Okay... well, I can see we will not agree on anything here tonight. Shall we just change the topic?"

"Fine by me. I don't know how Barrett works with you, Olivia!" Ari said, removing his arm from mine.

Barrett leaned forward. "Hey, Ari, don't fuck with Olivia... just a word of advice, pal. She's got bigger balls than you."

The entire table erupted into laughter while Francesca looked on, trying to play catchup.

"Yeah, no shit. How do you keep her in line?" Ari asked over the laughter.

"She holds her own." Barrett leaned behind Magnus, giving Olivia a knowing smile.

"Damn right I do." Olivia grinned at the size of the so-called balls she held, continuing the laughter around the table.

By the time dessert came around, Francesca had left Connor's side and wedged herself between Ari and me. Ari gladly spilled the beans—which designers were going broke, who to watch, and who was sleeping with who. After all, Ari had a Rolodex of models at his helm and a grandmother who was designer royalty.

"Pepper, who is your fav designer because this dress is seriously fierce?" Francesca asked, running the pad of her finger across the fabric.

"I have a few. I'm partial to Victoria Beckham, but with my hips, I struggle to get into her pencil skirts. So my go-tos are Emanuelle Freda, Lola, and Nable."

"Since the Kardashians, curves are back in, and anorexia is out." Ari winked at me.

I smiled, thanking him for the compliment. When he wasn't an asshole, he could be sweet.

"How can anyone like a ghetto booty? I mean, seriously, they must be implants. Gross," Francesca said, swinging her long mane of blonde hair behind her shoulder.

"How can anyone like skinny… no butt? It's like a fucking boy." Francesca gasped, perhaps because Ari was referring to exactly her shape. Tall, gorgeous, straight up and down, the typical size zero.

"Excuse me." I stood, pushing out my chair and excusing myself before getting in the middle of another situation. I walked past Lourde and Barrett, and she reached for my arm, stopping me.

"You okay, gorgeous?"

"Yes, nature calls." I steadied on, tilting my head to the side. Connor's piercing stare caused a warmth to scale my neck, and before a blush of crimson appeared on my cheeks, I disappeared through the velvet curtain and into the common area. Instead of the bathrooms, I walked outside to the sidewalk, desperate for fresh air.

Gazing up at the clear Manhattan night, the stars and Milky Way were bright and breathtaking, away from the light pollution over Times Square. I took a deep breath, filling my lungs completely before exhaling.

"Bit over-the-top in there, isn't it?" His gravelly voice shot a flurry of warmth throughout my body.

*Had he followed me out?*

I felt him hover close behind me. The heat of his skin radiated, warming mine. For fear of losing my composure, I kept my attention on the starry sky.

"It can be," I admitted.

He hovered close behind me. From my shadow, he shifted to stand beside me. When his arm brushed mine, I stilled.

"That is some dress," he growled. "Are you doing this to tease me?"

I turned to him. "Me, tease you?" I said, exasperated, having to endure Francesca's spindly fingers on him all night.

"Fair point."

I turned to stare outward.

"Why didn't you bring Jake?"

"He was busy tonight."

*Liar.*

I didn't want him here, not with my head in the clouds.

"I see," he said in a low voice.

"She's really something," I said, turning to him, and he stared at me, his eyes bright blue reflecting the street lamp.

"She is." He held my gaze to his. What did I expect him to say? *No, I'm not marrying her. I miss you?*

Fuck, I was so screwed. I cleared my throat. "Well, guess we should get back."

"Wait." He reached for my arm. His fingers wrapped around my wrist, and I stilled under his touch, trying to ignore what his touch did to my senses.

"What is it, Connor?"

"I... I think you're right. Let's go back," he said, loosening his grip around my wrist.

I nodded and offered a weak smile, shimmying my hips past him at a hasty pace that I knew he couldn't keep up with.

*What was he going to say?* Why did it matter?

I walked back inside, past full tables of the hip restaurant, ignoring the chatter. And was that a wolf whistle?

*What the hell?* Someone had brushed their hand across my ass. I spun around to find three men, one in particular whose hand was very close to me.

"That is some *asset* you got there, girl."

"What did you just say?"

It was as though a flash appeared. That's how quick it was. Connor appeared between me and the guy eye-fucking me like I was a ribeye steak.

He gripped the guy's shirt at the collar. "Don't you ever fucking touch her again."

I moved to the side. I could fight my own battles. But Connor's eyes were like poison, firing lasers into the dickhead who had manhandled me. The two guys on either side were now standing to help their comrade out.

"Chill, man, he was just playing."

"I don't give a fuck," Connor spat, pulling him tighter now. "She is a lady."

"Wearing that?" the fuckhead said, and I held my breath. *Oh God.*

"Connor, *no!*" I said, but it was too late.

He wielded his hand back and smashed it into the asshole's nose. A roaring crack sounded, followed by blood.

Gasps and squeals came from everywhere, and as I tried to separate Connor from the guy, I suddenly was pushed back, ending up on the floor. Not one to let a man fight battles for me, I pushed myself up off the floor, but when I stood up, I fell again.

"Ouch," I yelled out in pain. My ankle burned and ached.

Suddenly, Barrett, Magnus, and Ari surrounded the table.

"Pepper, are you okay?" Lourde and Olivia crowded down beside me.

"My ankle. I think I twisted it when I fell."

"Let me get some help." Olivia left as I tried poking my head up and over to see if Connor was okay.

Francesca was by his side, pulling him away from the commotion. "Stop this immediately!" she screamed out in distress. "There are cameras everywhere!"

Oh God, she was right. I looked around to see customers with their phones like it was a fucking concert, and we were the live act. Except Manhattan royalty was in a fistfight, and all because of me.

I put my head in my hands, my breath lodged in my throat. *Shit, what have I done?*

\* \* \*

Lourde insisted on taking me home, and after hobbling into bed, she sat beside me while Barrett waited in my living room.

"I'm sorry," I whispered, emotion clogging my throat.

"What are you sorry for? Those jerks shouldn't have laid a finger on you!"

## Lost Love

"I know, but the evening's ruined." An eruption of emotion engulfed my body, and wetness pricked behind my eyes. Then uncontrollable tears streamed down my cheeks.

"Oh, honey, why are you crying? You never cry!" She placed her hand on my arm, surprise etched on her porcelain face.

"I must be hormonal." I cried, overwhelmed at my sudden and rare onset of emotion.

The chimed sound of a message distracted me from full-blown crying. When I turned my phone over, his name appeared, and my breathing became rushed as my heart rate soared.

*Connor.*

Quickly, I picked it up, holding it in a way that shielded it from Lourde's view.

**Connor:** *Send them away, or I will.*

"What is it? You're blushing."

I looked up to find Lourde staring.

I let out a nervous laugh and turned my phone face down on the bed.

"It's Jake, isn't it? Are you guys working things out?"

"We're trying to, yes…" I agonized. But it wasn't exactly a lie. Certainly better than *your brother is stalking me, waiting for you to leave.*

The phone rang, and I lifted it quickly to my ear.

"Jake," I answered casually, but inwardly my heart thumped like a herd of elephants in the wild.

Connor groaned in frustration. "Get rid of them now, or I will." His razor-sharp tone sent shivers up my spine, taking me back to the dirty talk in the bedroom.

"Okay, okay, we're going!" Lourde said, getting up from the bed. "Keep the ice on that."

I placed my hand over the receiver. "I will, thanks, hun."

"Lunch tomorrow?"

"Okay." I'd agree to anything just to get her out of the apartment.

"Barrett, let's go," she yelled to him as she walked out of my bedroom.

"Bye, Pepper," Barrett shouted.

"Thanks!" I yelled back.

"Okay, they're going," I whispered into the phone just in case they could still hear me.

"I'll be right up," he said, then hung up.

*Damn! Sneaking around certainly made things fiery.*

Looking down, it dawned on me that I was still in my nude dress—the same dress that caused all of the commotion in the first place.

As quickly as I could manage, I wriggled to the edge of the bed, then hobbling over to my walk-in closet, I pulled out my favorite pajamas covered with the *Care Bears* cartoon. It was as sexy as a nun's habit. Perfect for *friends.*

Curling my arms around my mid-back, I located the dress zipper and tugged it down. Then, balancing on one foot, I wriggled the dress down my waist.

*Dammit.* It was stuck. I wrangled it, but the dress had folded over itself on my curves. I didn't have any time before the elevator pinged, and the doors opened.

"Pepper?" his voice echoed throughout the hallway.

*Shit!*

"Just a minute," I yelled and gave the dress one big yank off my hips. Losing my balance, I toppled over on my ankle. "Fuck!" I bit out in pain.

"What are you doing?" Connor appeared in the doorframe, his eyes like saucers.

Mortified, I looked down. Not only had I yanked the dress down, but the thin scrap of underwear I was wearing was now also around my knees as I shuffled to sit upright against the side of the bed.

My cheeks burned red, and peering up, I noticed him crouched down by my side, level with my naked tits. His gaze momentarily fell to my chest, and he let out a throaty sound. There was a fire in his eyes when they met mine. He leaned in, and my breath hitched in my throat. But instead of kissing me, his arm snaked around my waist in an attempt to lift me off the ground.

"Put your arms around me," he said in a low grumble, his brow slick with sweat.

*Oh my God.*

I did as he said, and he lifted me with one hand around my waist and the other around my bare ass. My body tingled at the connection as heat pooled in my core.

"Put me down, please, Connor." I sighed, absolutely mortified and aroused. It was an odd combination to be faced with.

He bent down, gently placing me on the bed. I was completely naked except for a bundled-up dress around my thighs as he stood above me. A fire burned behind his eyes, his Adam's apple bobbed in his throat as he swallowed. The air was electric.

"Fuck, Pepper, I ought to be mad at you, but seeing your body, it's hard to think of anything right now with my dick like lead."

I gasped, gazing down at the bulge in his pants. I wanted to reach out for it and caress him in my hands and take away his pain, his worry, and my frustrated feelings.

"Cover up before I claim you," he groaned out weakly before casting his fiery gaze across my breasts, down to my navel, and the straight line of black hair to my folds.

His hand left his side, reaching for my face. I leaned forward, my body betraying any morals I had left. But just before he touched me, he jerked back, stopping himself.

"Now, Pepper!" he commanded.

I exhaled loudly.

Watching him turn around, I clung to my last shred of dignity and reached for the throw next to me. He paced the length of my bedroom with his jaw set and rigid body. He appeared to berate himself for what could have happened a moment ago had he not held himself back.

With my heart jackhammering in my chest, I tossed the throw on top of my naked body, sure to cover myself up completely.

"Okay." I breathed out in a whisper. "I'm covered."

He stopped pacing and turned around, then adjusted himself and sat beside me, his gaze falling on my exposed swollen ankle.

"Did you just fall again?"

"I was trying to get changed into my pajamas," I admitted, thinking that maybe rushing wasn't such a brilliant idea after all. My plan to wear my ugliest but comfiest pajamas had failed miserably, and he'd seen all of me again.

"These fancy ones?" He held up my pajama bottoms.

"Hey," I cautioned. "They're my favorite."

"Are they Care Bears?"

"Don't knock it till you watch it."

"I have. Lourde loved the Care Bears growing up. I was more into Masters of the Universe!"

I laughed, and any trace of humiliation had soon left the room.

"Let me help you. After all, I'm the one who got you in this situation."

"I can do it," I said, reaching for the pants out of his grasp.

"No, you can't." He flung them away and out of my reach. "Argue with me and I'll have to strap you to the bed."

*I might like that.*

"Pepper…"

"What?" I rolled my lips in, my chest rising and falling at the idea of his ties binding my hands together.

"There's nothing more I'd like to see than you tied up with one of my neckties. But if you look at me like that again, I promise you it won't end well."

"Okay," I breathed out on a sigh.

"I'm engaged, I can't go back from that." His hand went underneath the blanket, his thumb brushing my thigh as he pushed the rest of my dress and thong down past my ankles. I remained silent, letting him undress me.

I felt weak around him, my body buckling to his touch. As I took him in, torment stretched across the tightness in his jaw and the stiffness in his neck. He, too, was affected, fighting this just as much as me.

He reached for my bottoms and threaded them carefully around my sore ankle, then the other, before sliding them up my legs and past my knees. I lifted off the bedsheet and his fingers brushed past my thighs, causing me to take a sudden sharp breath when he reached the curve of my ass.

I cleared my throat. "Thank you."

His hands lingered around the sides of my thighs, his face close to mine. A war played out behind his eyes.

I turned to quickly reach for the pajama shirt flinging it over my head and chest, then I gazed up to find him unmoving in his stare. Silence stretched out between us, and I ached for him to touch me. He tilted his head down, his lips parting.

"Go home to your fiancée, Connor." I eventually bit out.

He moved back, creating space between us. "She's not at my home."

"Well, maybe she ought to be." I pulled up the blanket so it covered my shoulders.

"I just came to see that you're okay," he said, his gaze sincere.

"Those guys were jerks, but nothing I couldn't handle by myself."

"You're welcome," he muttered.

"I didn't ask for your help, Connor. Now look at what's happened. It's already in the media. Your father—"

"Fuck him. Anyone with an iPhone could see I was helping you."

"You need to forget about me like I need to forget about you," I said, my voice slightly raised. "You need to focus on Francesca and the life you're having with her. I don't think we can be friends anymore."

"I did this for you tonight. Don't turn this around to be about us."

"That's the point. There is no us! We had fun while it lasted. I used you to get over Jake, and now we're back together…" I picked up an invisible speck of lint on the duvet.

*God, are we even back together?*

"You've fucked him, haven't you?"

"That's none of your business. Do I ask you if you've slept with Francesca?"

"Well, I haven't." He jumped up and started pacing the length of my bedroom.

"What is it you want, Connor? You're so messed up I don't even think you know."

"Don't do this, Pepper. I need you in my life."

"I don't think we can ever be friends, Connor. We've crossed that line, and I'm working on my relationship with Jake. We're just a scandal waiting to happen. And I'm sure you've landed yourself in another one of those tonight by punching the jerk at the restaurant."

"You're right." He paced back and forth, his head and shoulders slumped to the ground. "Tell me something then… why do I miss you like crazy?" He closed his eyes momentarily, sucking in a lungful of air. "You're all I think about, Pepper."

My heart ached, and my body crumpled in on itself. But as seconds passed, I bristled, anger rising in my chest.

"You don't miss me, Connor. You miss my body," I

declared. "Please see yourself out." I didn't dare look at him because if I did, I'd meet his steely blues, and I knew my resolve would falter. So instead, I pulled the blanket up and tucked my head into my knees.

After a few seconds, I heard his footsteps grow fainter, followed by the ping of the elevator.

I needed to call Jake. No more half-assed attempt to patch things up. Connor was gone, and Jake was my sole focus.

He had to be.

## 15

## CONNOR

I had to walk away. Leave Pepper's apartment because she told me to. If she hadn't, I honestly don't know if I would have left of my own volition.

I had thoughts—impure thoughts—when my eyes raked down the curves of her body. But she didn't deserve that, and neither did Francesca.

I pressed the accelerator on my Porsche Cayenne, and it thundered down Third Avenue until the inevitable traffic hit. I slammed my hand down on the steering wheel, pressing the brake suddenly.

*Fuck.* I was so messed up.

Punching that jerk had consequences. The way he touched her ass like he had some claim to it curdled my blood. I didn't have another choice. *Did I?*

Everything should be fine. I had an attractive fiancée, I was CEO of the largest American media company, and I had all the toys money could buy. I had nothing to complain about. *Then why did everything feel upside down and inside out?*

The car horn sounded behind me, and when I looked up, the lights were green.

## Lost Love

"Fuck you!" I yelled out the window, my rage barely containable. It felt like at any moment, I could snap. My foot pressed the pedal until it hit the floor, and channeling my inner Lewis Hamilton, I swerved through traffic until I reached my garage.

I hit end on the fourth call from Alfred that interrupted the "Rage Against the Machine" song blaring through my car speakers. *TMZ* had splashed the news, but fuck it, I didn't need to take his call. I'd deal with it tomorrow.

I took the private elevator from my garage to my penthouse, and when the doors opened, something was amiss. *I hadn't left the lights on, had I?*

Christ, Alfred better not be here. He'd only ever been here once, and that was for business. He had no interest in me. That much was clear.

"Honey. Is that you?" Her voice hit me like a migraine, and I pulled in a lungful of air.

*What the fuck.*

Francesca rounded the corner, holding a half-empty glass of bubbles.

"I see you've made yourself at home. How did you get in?"

"Your concierge recognized me... thought it was odd your *fiancée* didn't have a key to your apartment."

*Well, he's fired.*

"I tried calling," she offered, aware of my lukewarm reception.

I walked into the kitchen, threw my keys and wallet on the counter, and headed to the bar. Pouring myself a whiskey, I gulped it down in one lug, the warmth sliding down my throat.

"Where did you go?" Her tone was terse, almost obtuse.

"I had a few things to attend to." I poured another drink, then walked over, collapsing on the armchair.

"At eleven at night?"

I nodded, not caring to elaborate.

"I see."

When I looked up, she was in front of me. Bending down, she placed her legs on either side of mine, so she was straddling me, and my dick sprang to life.

I groaned.

*This was wrong. So wrong.*

She clasped my face, and I put my hand up to hers, pulling it back down.

"What is it you want, Francesca?" I asked, feeling confused and defeated.

*What was wrong with me?* Here was a beautiful woman on my lap, grinding on my dick, and I was too much of a pussy to fuck her?

"I want you to fuck me, Connor. Why else do you think I'm here?"

I laughed. "Shit! I don't know, maybe to talk? See how my new role as CEO is going? Have you once asked me about that?"

She leaned forward. Her glossy lips brushed my neck, and I wrestled with the emotions.

"Relax," she breathed out in a whisper.

I closed my eyes. An image of Pepper's black curls and chocolate eyes immediately came to mind. Her velvet mouth traced my neck, down my jaw, and I groaned out. Maybe I could go through with this if I just thought about Pepper. Hands clawed at my chest, slowly unbuttoning my shirt, and I tried to ignore the clicking of nails. Her lips nipped my jawline, sucking and panting with each kiss. My balls clenched, and my dick thickened at my seam, then I felt the tug of my belt buckle.

"That's it, just relax." Immediately, I was pulled out of my Pepper wet dream with a voice that cut razor-sharp.

*Fuck, no.*

Francesca's voice shook me out of my Pepper coma, and I

jerked back into the armchair. My hands fell around her wrists, stopping her from unbuckling my pants.

"What the fuck, Connor?" she barked, her face blooming with anger.

"Not tonight."

"Well, your dick says otherwise," she said, slipping her leg off me to stand and nearly losing her balance.

I slid my hand down my pants and adjusted my strained cock. "I have a lot on at work."

"That's twice you've turned me down." She smoothed down her dress with a jerky movement. "You've never turned me down," she said, pushing out her chest so her latest breast enlargement was on full display.

"I know, it's not you. It's me."

*Fuck, did I just say that?*

She bent her hand to her hip. "You're kidding, right?"

"Fuck, Francesca. What do you want from me?" I threw back the rest of my whiskey in one go, but it did little to settle the unease.

"What I want is to get laid by my fiancée. Jesus, is that too much to ask? Or is this something that will need to be written into the prenup along with every other condition?"

"It has been arranged since we were kids, Francesca. It doesn't mean we have to consummate it."

"Are you listening to yourself? You're one of the biggest players in Manhattan, and you're telling me you don't want to consummate things?"

"That is exactly what I'm telling you." *Although, my dick has other thoughts.*

"Well, then, so what, are we meant to exist like this, having separate bedrooms and taking lovers on the side because you're not meeting my needs?"

I exhaled. It would be exactly what my parents had—a lackluster marriage. I didn't want that. I really didn't want what they had. I owed it to her to give it a shot, at least. *Right?*

"No, I guess that's not what I want."

"Good." She crossed her arms over, then slowly walked back over.

"That's not what I want either."

She huffed out. "Let me take you out to dinner. Let's try to do this properly."

"A date? You want to take your fiancée out on a date?"

Instead of being grateful, she looked at me like I just asked to lick out her asshole.

"That's exactly what I'm proposing."

"Well, at least there's one proposal… fine, text me where and when."

She turned, put down her champagne flute, and snatched her bag, walking toward the elevator.

"I'll do that."

She stopped walking and turned abruptly.

"Just for the record, I'm not fucking happy, Connor." She eyeballed me with over-arching eyebrows.

"I have needs, Connor, and if you can't meet them, then there are others who can. Many others."

If she was trying to make me jealous, it wasn't working. "I'm sure there are," I added.

"Well, goodbye, *hubby.*"

I didn't bother with a response. My fate was well and truly sealed. I best make the most of it.

\* \* \*

I didn't give a fuck who saw us argue. I probably should have, but I just didn't care. Caring about my old man disappeared when I realized he valued his precious company and legacy more than his son.

## Lost Love

I was a smart kid. I excelled at everything I tried my hand at. I pushed myself for the sole purpose of gaining my father's respect and attention. After I realized it wasn't coming, I stopped trying. That's when alcohol became my secret poison, and I abused it.

That's when I woke up naked on the corner and secretly probably wanted to get my old man's attention. That was on me. That was all on me. I knew all that, so then why was he still fucking with me?

Why couldn't I disengage from the man he was? Why am I watching him, flushed with anger, hurling every expletive under the sun from across my desk and silently reveling because I pissed him off?

"Are you smiling?" he asked, slamming his hands on my desk.

I sucked in a lungful of air.

"You know, Alfred, you come in here, screaming at me for making the front page of the news, and you haven't even asked me what happened."

"It doesn't matter what happened." He threw the *Daily Sun* at me, and it bounced off my chest, falling into my lap.

I picked it up and flapped it back into shape. Someone had photographed me in an anger-infused rage, holding Casper Knight by the collar, the dickhead who felt up Pepper.

Probably not my finest hour. But I stood tall and muscular against the little pipsqueak who thought he had a claim over a woman walking in the crowd.

"But it does actually matter. All the little details if you care to look and focus on anything but you and your legacy for once."

"Do you even care that the share price has dropped nearly twenty percent today as America wakes up to the news that its newly appointed CEO has assault charges leveled at him?"

*That motherfucker. That would explain the many calls from the family lawyers I let go to voicemail.*

"He was the one assaulting Pepper." I exclaimed. "She was walking back to the table, and I was behind her when this fuckwit decided he owned a piece of her ass."

"So you decided to punch him out, is that it? Tell me, son, why were you with Pepper and not with Francesca?"

"What?"

"You've been spending lots of time with Pepper, and as far as I can remember, Pepper is Lourde's friend, not yours."

My neck itched with a burning heat. *Did the old man have me followed?*

"How would you know that?"

"I know everything." He looked at me seriously. "End whatever the fuck you have going on with Pepper now, or all of this is gone."

I slammed my fist down on the table. *Fuck him.*

"We are friends. That's all."

He stood slowly. "Friends with women we've fucked isn't possible."

"I'm not taking relationship advice from a man who's not happy in his."

"Happiness is bought, and your mother is very comfortable."

I shook my head. "But she's not happy, and neither are you."

He raised his finger, leveling it at me. "Listen here, Francesca's family and ours have a lot to gain from this union. The legacy will be fruitful for generations to come. There are benefits to this union that go beyond your dick and its needs."

"So what? I'm meant to take one for the team here? What if I don't want to?"

He blinked as though he didn't understand the question.

The silence between us grew uncomfortable before he expelled a breath. "As Diamonds, we don't have options, son."

His steady eye contact reflected the tiniest bit of comfort in the unvarnished truth that was my future.

I knew he was right. We might be one of the wealthiest families in the United States, but that came at a cost. A responsibility that decades ago had been set in stone by my granddad.

"I know," I groaned.

He nodded and turned, giving me his back, and headed for the door.

"Just so you know, I'm not sorry I punched out that asshole for Pepper."

He turned to face me. *Was that empathy in his weathered eyes? Don't be delusional, Connor. His heart was harder than steel.*

"Oh, I know."

## 16

## PEPPER

My phone vibrated in my purse, and as I hobbled toward the café entrance, I slid it out, only to be let down.

"Hey, Jake."

"Pepper, angel, sorry I haven't called sooner. Work has been on my ass like a rash."

"That's okay," I said, gingerly taking a seat at the corner table.

"Eventful dinner?"

"Sure was. I guess you saw the news?"

"Connor got himself into trouble again, according to *TMZ*," Jake said, laughing down the line.

"He did because he was defending me, Jake."

"Really? What happened?"

"I'm fine, but some lowlife decided he owned part of my ass and touched me without my consent."

"Touched you on your ass?"

"He squeezed it when I walked by."

There was silence at the other end. "And?"

"And what?"

"Is that all?"

"What do you mean? Is that all?" I fumed at his casual attitude toward the incident. The same incident Connor put his reputation on the line by defending me.

"You're a big girl. You can handle it."

My jaw tightened. *Okay, maybe see it from his side, Pepper.*

"I know I can," I stated, void of emotion.

"Exactly, so why all the fuss?"

"Well, Connor saw it happen and told the guy to back off, then an argument ensued, and I got pushed back, hurt my ankle, and now the asshole is suing Connor for smashing up his already ugly face."

"Well, Connor shouldn't have assaulted him."

"But he should have squeezed my ass?" I twirled the end of my hair, exasperated.

He sighed out. "That's just what guys do, especially when they're with their friends."

"Geez. It's nice to know where you stand on the issue. Well, anyway, I have to run. I'm meeting Lourde now. Oh, and thank you for your concern," I rasped with sarcasm.

"Pepper, angel, I don't mean it that way."

"Sure you don't."

"Are we still on for dinner tomorrow night? I booked your favorite restaurant in West Soho."

I promised myself I'd try with Jake. We had a history. I owed it to us to work on it, and it was the best Italian in all of Manhattan.

"Yes, fine." *Whatever.* "Lourde's here. I have to run."

"Love you," he said.

I almost laughed out loud. "Yeah, I'm not there yet, Jake."

"Okay, okay."

I hung up the phone, more irritated than when I answered his call. Picking up the menu, I vacantly stared at the piece of paper while silently fuming.

What kind of man didn't stand up for his woman? Yes, I could stand up for myself, and I did, but there was something noble about a man going to the ends of the earth for his woman. Call me traditional, but I'd want my boyfriend to give a fuck if someone else was touching my ass.

"What will it be?" The server had her trusty pad and pen at the helm.

"Espresso. Actually, make it a double shot," I said. "And I'll order for my friend who'll be here any minute. She'll have an English breakfast tea… hold the milk."

I'd used Lourde's arrival as an excuse to end the phone call. If I hadn't, I was a breath away from telling him to fuck off completely.

"Done." With a trusty smile, the server retreated.

I put my ankle up on the third seat. It hurt having walked on it from the Uber to the café out front of Barrett's building where Lourde worked.

"Sorry I'm late, the kitchen designer had to redo her plans and couldn't do it without me." Lourde slid into the red leather seat opposite, looking suitably polished, with her hair pulled back in a high chignon.

"No sweat. I've ordered you tea."

"Excellent. How's the foot?" She glanced down at my elevated foot perched on the seat. "What are you wearing shiny red heels for? Are you insane?"

"Certified." We both chuckled. "You know I love heels too much to part with them for just a sore ankle. Which is most likely a sprain, I might add."

The server appeared, setting down our coffee and tea.

"Thank you." I took the espresso to my lips, needing an instant pick-me-up.

"Did you order any of those pastries in the window?" Lourde asked.

"What pastries?" I took a sip, the coffee sliding down my throat.

The server let out a giggle. "You're joking, right?" Lourde eyeballed me, prompting me to turn and seek out the mystery pastries.

The entire front window was filled top to bottom in pastries. I don't know how I'd missed it. I let out a laugh.

"What? I was on the phone with Jake when I walked in!"

"Well, that explains it then." She turned to the server. "We'll take the pain au chocolat and the apple strudel."

"Both good choices." The server retreated, and I was already salivating.

"So what happened last night was crazy, right? Seriously, my poor brother, I don't know what's worse, dealing with an assault charge or having to deal with Dad."

"It's terrible." I shook my head.

"I wish Dad wasn't so tough on him. He's not like that with me, only Connor. I don't understand it." She sighed. "Anyway, Connor's a big boy."

*Yes, he is.* I couldn't help it. My mind went *there*.

"You know Olivia and I are giving our own business some more thought."

"You are? That sounds great! You guys would kill it. You know it's so difficult to find quality interior decorators."

"Especially designers who cater to the high-end clientele… and with my contacts, we could do *really* well."

"Do it!"

She fidgeted with the corner of the menu. "We'd be leaving Barrett in a hole."

"Well, do it when you have a plan, and you're not leaving Barrett in a hole."

"We're working on it."

"Does he know?"

"Of course. Nothing is off-limits with us. We're an open book."

"How sweet," I said, and it came out a little sarcastic, which I had not intended.

She side-eyed me. "How's everything with Jake?"

"A work in progress."

"You know I'm your biggest advocate, so I'm going to say this, with love... sometimes flogging a dead horse isn't worth it."

"I know, but I really haven't tried." I let out a sigh. "If I'm honest, I've been a little distracted," I admitted rather sheepishly.

She narrowed her eyes. "Does this have to do with the one-night stand from a few weeks ago at my housewarming?"

"Possibly. But you know me. I don't kiss and tell."

"Goddammit! Tell me everything. No wonder you've been reluctant to patch things up with Jake."

"No, honestly, it's not like that. That guy... well, he was just a way to get over Jake. He used me too, and we both knew what we were doing."

"And now?"

"And now, it's over," I said, leaving the sentence to hang in the air.

"It doesn't sound like it's over."

"It's complicated."

"Do you like him more than a fuck?"

At that moment, the server appeared with two plates, and we both laughed.

The server let out a slight smile before setting down the pastries and quickly walked away.

"Do I like him more than fuck?" I repeated the question. "Of course, I do."

"Then go after him!"

"I can't."

"What, why?" she asked, exasperated with my response. Except no one was more exasperated and frustrated at this whole situation than me.

*He's your brother, and he's engaged!*

"Like I said, it's complicated. I just have to move on."

"And settle for second best?"

"I'm not settling. I'm trying to fix things with Jake."

"Uh-huh?" she said, reaching for the pain au chocolat and taking a large bite. "Girl, you know I love you like a sister, and you know I'm here for you. When you want to tell me, tell me."

*Sister. Hell, I hadn't even thought of that benefit. What? Stop. Now you're thinking of Connor as your husband. Oh my God. What the…*

"You okay?"

"Huh?" I looked up to find Lourde staring at me. If only she could read my mind. "Yes, fine."

"Just promise me you won't settle. You're too goddamn important to just settle."

I reached for the Danish and tore it in half. Divided, damaged, and torn. Divided between what was right and what was wrong and not wanting to settle as Lourde said. But let's face it. I was damaged. My trust broken. Torn between a man I can't have and a man that I have a history with.

I nodded. "You know I will." I popped the flakey pastry in my mouth, enjoying the buttery goodness.

"In the meantime, there's been something I've been meaning to ask you."

Fuck, it was delicious. I stuffed the next piece into my mouth. "What's that?"

"Will you be my maid of honor?"

"Hell, yes!" I shouted with a mouthful of pastry. I leaped up, putting weight on my sore ankle to embrace her. Lourde stood to meet me, and I flung my arms around her. We squealed like school kids as we hugged it out, jumping up and down on the spot.

Eventually, my ankle ached, and I let her go. "I think we caused quite a spectacle!" she said, casting her eyes around the cafe.

"Who cares! I can't believe you left it till the end of our meetup to ask me that!"

She laughed a cheeky laugh. "Come on, let's get out of here."

After pulling out the money to cover our bill, I placed it on the table, then shouldered my purse. We walked out of the café onto the busy street.

"So, who else is in the bridal party?"

"I asked you first, but next, I'll call Grace… that's if she will ever come back from the Hamptons!"

"I know, right? Damn, I miss her… who else?"

"Olivia."

"Oh, I really like her," I gushed. "Especially when she stood her ground with Ari."

"I know. She's fiery as fuck."

"What's her story anyway?"

"All I know is she's worked her ass off to get where she is. She came from very humble beginnings, and that's pretty much Olivia. Hey, can you walk a little?"

"Sure, just a little," I said, taking her arm for support and rounding the corner. "Well, I'm so happy we're all bridesmaids together. It's going to be one epic wedding!"

"And my fourth bridesmaid is Evelyn."

"Evelyn Black, Barrett's sister from Boston?"

"Yes. Oh, hun, that's so sweet. I had a brief chat with her at the charity ball, and she seemed so lovely."

"Yeah, she's a gem. I'm trying to convince her to come live out here."

"What's stopping her?"

"She has the best doctors and help where she is in Boston.

Her local hospital and doctors have been fantastic in her treatment for her permanent injuries."

"Surely, Barrett could fly them out?"

"Of course, in a heartbeat, he'd do anything for his sister, but she's reluctant to leave all her friends. Anyway, let's just say I'm working on it."

"I can't wait. Have you set a date yet?"

We slowed down in front of a store. When I looked up, I realized it was a familiar name.

"Not yet. Wait. Isn't this the lingerie store we visited in the Hamptons?" Lourde asked, noticing the same discrete signage and blacked-out windows we saw in East Hampton.

"Oooh, it is!" I said. My excitement suddenly waned when I realized the lingerie bought in the Hamptons was just for Jake.

"What is it?"

"It's just I bought all this lacey stuff for Jake, and now, I can't comprehend why he'd do what he did with her."

"I can't either." She gripped my hand.

"Sorry, this is so not important right now when we are talking about you."

I shook away my sadness. But I wasn't sad about Jake. Rather it was that both my men had found someone else. And suddenly, I felt like the backup option.

"We don't have to go in," Lourde said.

"Don't be ridiculous. We have to go in. We need to get you something for your wedding night!" Without waiting for a reply, I pressed the doorbell.

"And maybe if it doesn't work out with Jake, you can find something in here for your fuck- buddy."

I laughed. Hell, there was no harm in looking. Was there?

"If you insist," I muttered, and the heavy door swung open.

\* \* \*

"You look hot!" Jake said, staring across at me from the corner table in the Italian restaurant.

Something derailed his grand plans to pick me up again, so I had to make my own way into Soho.

He looked handsome, but that didn't matter. Being half an hour late, I nearly emptied my third glass of Chianti, and if it weren't for the homemade bread I'd been holing out, I would have left already.

"Thanks," I said, turning my head, so he kissed my cheek.

"I'm sorry I'm late. Work ran late, and then the Manhattan traffic. You know what it's like, honey."

He sat down and picked up the menu.

Doubt lingered in my mind. Doubt *he* put there by cheating on me with another woman after our year together.

"What were you working on?" I questioned. I had never asked him about his work before, so I watched him for any telltale signs that he was not telling the truth.

"Bit of this and that. I was in my strategy meeting when it ran over, though," he said, eyeballing the menu.

"Uh-huh." I huffed out. The server appeared, and we placed our order.

I reached for my wine when Jake's hand wrapped around mine. "I'm so glad we are doing this." His blue eyes met mine.

"Me too," I admitted.

"Maybe this can be the start of something fresh."

"Yes, a fresh start." *I need that. I needed to forget Connor Diamond.*

"I want that with you, Pepper."

The server appeared. "Ah, *he's* arrived. What can I get you?"

I think the server felt sorry for me, giving me my third

Chianti on the house because she thought I was being stood up. *Sweetheart.*

Jake looked at me, then to the server, trying to dissect the girl code between us.

"I'll just have a red wine."

"Would you like to pick one from the list, sir? We have loads to pick from," she said, directing him to the backside of the menu.

"Do you want me to pick you one?" I offered, but he let out an exasperated huff, ignoring me, and scanned the menu.

I offered the waitress a meek, apologetic smile.

A shriek pulled my attention away from Jake as a tall, thin woman walked toward me.

"Look who's here!" Francesca exclaimed, the entire restaurant turning toward the commotion.

I looked behind her, and there he stood, a serious expression across his blue eyes, still in his suit from work.

His blue eyes hit mine with an intensity that sent butterflies in my stomach to wake up from their slumber.

*Fuck me.*

"Francesca, hi!" I offered, meeting her enthusiasm.

"And this must be your boyfriend Lourde told me about."

"Jake," Jake volunteered, standing up immediately.

The server moved away, and Jake stood, staring at the beauty in front of him. In a tight dress, she left little to the imagination—breasts pushed to the sun and a tight-fitting short terracotta-colored dress that showed off her pencil-thin legs.

"Well, aren't you handsome?" she said, pulling him in for an air kiss.

Connor appeared beside Francesca, staring at me like I'd done something wrong. Staring at me like he wanted to punish me by handcuffing me to the wall and doing bad things to me. I'd seen that look before, and I caved under his stare.

"Connor," I said, breaking the awkwardness between us.

He pulled me in for a tight embrace, his hands falling around the shell of my hip and squeezing me ever so gently. His lips dusted my cheek, awfully close to my mouth.

"Pepper," he said, his voice low before releasing his grip on me.

My skin burned where his touch left my body. Why hadn't Jake made me feel like that?

I felt Jake's glare. "Sorry I'm being rude. Connor, this is Jake, my... um... boyfriend," I eventually said to the surprised but cheerful look on Jake.

"I've seen you at a few parties, but I don't think we've been introduced." Connor extended his arm, and Jake shook it.

I watched the two men I'd been intimate with. Jake was a boy compared to Connor. His height alone was enough to eclipse Jake, not that Jake was short, but Connor exuded strength with his broad shoulders and unwavering confidence.

The server stepped in. "Would you like to sit together?" she offered, taking in Connor not so subtly.

"Yes!" Jake and Francesca said at the same time.

I let out a laugh. It was beyond ludicrous, the four of us on a date together.

Jake turned toward me. "What?" I shrugged. I sided up to Jake and whispered in his ear. "Are you sure you don't just want to sit together with me?"

"No, why? We're all friends here."

"Uh-huh?" I turned to see Connor piercing bullets into my back. What the fuck had I done to him? He was engaged, not me.

We made our way to the bar while the server sorted the table settings. Francesca and Jake were enamored in conversation. I smiled politely, utterly oblivious to their discussion, while vacantly staring at Connor, who had already ordered and downed a shot of whiskey, ignoring me altogether.

"Table's ready," Connor deadpanned and marched toward it.

*What was his deal?* It wasn't my idea to sit together.

We returned to a set table, where Jake sat beside me, with Connor taking a seat opposite me and Francesca at his side, opposite Jake. I pretended to pick from the menu while Francesca and Jake spoke about the latest tabloid scandals and how they knew the same people in the same circles.

Glancing up from the menu, I emptied my glass of wine.

"So, do you know what you want?" Connor asked. He looked at me like he wasn't breathing, and I blinked, having to repeat his question in my head.

When I didn't respond, a slight smile tipped the edge of his lips. "To eat, Pepper."

I laughed nervously. "I probably should know. I've been waiting half an hour for Jake here." My hand came up to his cheek in a playful slap.

I noticed the vein in Connor's neck tick and his jaw pulled tight.

"Honey, I told you I was held up."

"What is it that held you up, Jake?" Connor asked pointedly, and I pulled my hand down.

"What is this, the FBI?" Jake laughed off the question.

*Why was he asking him that anyway? It wasn't his business why he was late.*

Francesca laughed alongside Jake. "Connor, I'm hungry. Let's order." Francesca called over the same server to our table in a rude hand gesture that had me shrinking into the back of my chair.

"What can I get you?" the server asked.

"I'll have the green salad," Francesca replied, slamming the menu shut.

"And for your entrée?"

"That's it." Francesca squinted at the server in confusion.

I looked at Jake, whose gaze leveled on Francesca's set of tits. I cleared my throat, and he stared at me like a deer in the headlights.

"That's how you stay so slim!" Jake said, diverting his gaze to Francesca.

"Why, thank you, Jake. At least someone appreciates me." She tilted her head down toward Connor.

Maybe they weren't sleeping together after all. I ignored the fizzle in my belly.

"I'll have—"

"Ladies first, Jake," Connor interjected in a stern but friendly tone.

Jake grimaced. "Of course. Pepper, what are you having?"

"I'll have the creamy pappardelle with extra parmesan."

Francesca giggled. "Aren't you worried about calories?"

The server glanced down at me and widened her eyes.

"Not at all," I admitted.

"Excellent choice." The server smiled. "The homemade pappardelle is our specialty."

"I'll have the steak well done, no sauce, no onions," Jake said.

"Are you writing this down somewhere?"

"It's all up here." The server pointed to her head.

"Huh." Francesca slid her hand onto Connor's thigh and momentarily saw him wince at the contact.

"Steak rare with all the sides."

"Well, you're both hungry, aren't you?" Francesca giggled.

*In more ways than one.*

Connor glanced at me before putting his hand behind her shoulders.

The server retreated but not before throwing me a so-sorry-for-suggesting-you-join-tables stare.

I smiled, *think nothing of it.* But really, I didn't want to be here, especially pretending to be in this perfect loved-up relationship when it felt like anything but.

Especially when Connor's touch did things to me that Jake hadn't in the year we were together.

\*\*\*

"How's your salad?" I asked Francesca after I watched her pick out the cheese and just eat the greens. Hell, I was starving just looking at her.

"So, how long have you guys been together?" Francesca just ignored her like she hadn't spoken.

"Ten months," Jake said, leaning over to kiss me. His lips hastily brushed mine in the first kiss we'd had on the mouth in a long time. Pity it had to be like this—for show.

"It's actually closer to thirteen months, but who's counting," I said, taking the napkin to my mouth. When I glanced up at Connor, I was desperately seeking a reaction to the kiss. What I wasn't expecting was a fire in his eyes that burned angrily behind his blue eyes.

Was he jealous of Jake? Surely not. He had royalty next to him. Francesca put her hand on his thigh, stroking it back and forth under the table. She did nothing to hide her movements.

The idea of these two in bed made me nearly physically ill. I looked down at my half-eaten creamy pasta, suddenly feeling unwell.

"Excuse me," I said, pulling out my chair.

"Hun, you okay? You don't look so well?" Jake asked.

"Yes, fine." I smiled weakly, but I needed to get out of this situation and stat.

I rushed off to the bathroom, burying my head in my hands as I sat in the stall.

*What the fuck? Be cool, Pepper. Be cool.*

Jake loves you. He is here for you. Focus on that. Focus on

him even though he seemed less interested in me and more interested in Francesca's huge basketballs.

He's a guy. All guys like boobs. I pushed away the thought. *You're only feeling like this because Connor's here.*

Black polished shoes stopped in front of the stall. *Connor.*

"Let me in, Pepper."

*Oh my.*

"Connor?" I stood, unlocking the door.

He quickly pushed me inside and locked the door behind him.

"What are you doing? Francesca could walk in here at any moment."

"I came to see if you're okay."

I stared at him. The intensity in his eyes changed from sky blue to dark indigo. He stood over me, so close I could see the pulse in his neck pounding.

"I'm fine," I admitted, trying to step away from him but hitting the back of the toilet seat. He'd cornered me, and now I couldn't breathe.

"He's no good for you, Pepper."

"Excuse me?"

"You heard me."

I blinked, unsure I heard him correctly. "You have no right to tell me that."

He pushed a hair behind my ear, tilting my face up to meet his. "Does he make you scream like I do? Does he know every part of your body like I do?"

I exhaled, breathing out. "Connor… please."

He lowered his head to mine. "Can he make you wet with just one kiss?"

"Connor," I whispered. I trailed his face with my hand, and he squeezed his eyes closed. "Can she make you feel like I can?"

Suddenly, he opened his eyes. "Not even close." He

slammed his lips on mine, his chest and arms enveloping me in an intoxicatingly forbidden kiss.

I opened my mouth for him without hesitation, wanting him like he needed me. Warmth pooled between my legs as he gripped my waist tightly, his fingers dragging to the front of my navel. I inhaled sharply.

Fuck! I was that other woman, the woman I swore I could never be.

I pulled away sharply. "Connor, we can't," I said breathlessly.

Shocked, he took me in, then took in his surroundings. Had he just realized what we'd done? He was engaged, for fuck's sake.

He growled. "Fuck, I shouldn't have done that."

"No, you shouldn't have," I admitted, my body completely betraying me and leaning into him. But I was angry, so angry at him.

"Why are you inked on my mind, Pepper?"

He leaned his forehead on mine. "I'm not the other woman, Connor. I can't be what comes between you and your fiancée."

He scanned my face while his hand glided down, tracing my cheekbones to my bottom lip. I clenched my eyes closed. A moment later, his hand left, then there was a click.

I opened my eyes to watch him walk away, leaving me in a tangled mess.

# 17

## CONNOR

When she returned to the table, it was as though the kiss had never happened.

"You okay, Pepper?" Francesca asked, completely oblivious to what had just happened.

Guilt washed over me like an oil spill. I shouldn't have put Pepper in this situation. Rather, I should accept my role of fiancé to the annoying woman beside me. But the way she looked up at me and the feel of her hand on my face was enough to push me over the edge.

"Yes, thanks," Pepper said, smiling and not meeting my gaze. "They cleared the main dishes?" Pepper asked.

"I didn't think you'd want the rest," Jake admitted.

"But why?" Pepper stared at Jake, waiting for a response. When he shrugged and ignored her question, I wanted to reach over the table and shake him to his senses. Beside him was a devastatingly gorgeous, intelligent woman, screaming to be treated like a princess, and he was seriously ignoring her. I wondered what she saw in the limp dick in the first place.

"Who's up for dessert?"

"No," Pepper and I said at the same time.

Jake's eyes widened. "Really? You're always up for dessert."

"Still not feeling great, that's all," she added, smoothing it over.

I watched Jake rest his arm around her neck and pull her into him. Her head fell to his shoulder awkwardly, and my muscles bunched as I balled my hands into fists on my thighs at the sight.

"Would you mind if I had something?" he asked her.

Pepper nestled into his chest further, and I did everything in my power not to reach over the table and pull him off her. "Sure, get what you want," she admonished.

Excellent. "While you were on your phone call, Jake and I already chose the souffle and the frozen berry compote with the honeycomb bomb."

"Okay, great," I said, feigning some level of excitement.

Francesca repeated the order to the server, who dutifully took it back to the kitchen.

"Connor, how is it now that you've taken over from your father?" Jake asked, patting down his shirt.

"It's great," I said, not wanting to talk about my life, especially with Jake.

"Oh, don't be modest." Francesca patted me on the shoulder like a fucking dog. "He's going to take this company into the modern age."

I ran a hand through my hair, turning to Francesca. It was the first time she'd ever discussed my position, and now she was answering for me?

"What? That's what Daddy says." She stared at her manicure.

"And how does the Duke know what I'm up to?" My skin prickled with unease. "Oh." I let out a sigh. His stake in Diamond Incorporated doubled the moment the announcement of our engagement went public.

"Sounds difficult," Jake remarked, stroking Pepper's arm. I

noticed her still at the connection, which sent a warmth radiating through my chest.

I sniffed. "Does it?"

"Well, you have your father's reputation to live up to. I can't imagine what that would be like."

"What is it you do again, Jake?"

Pepper jerked upright. "Jake is a third-year medical student doing his rotation at Manhattan General Hospital."

My stomach hardened. What was she playing at? Well, two could play.

I smiled. "I bet those nurses take special care of their doctors."

Jake let out a laugh. Pepper's features bloomed into a scowl. Even angry, she looked so fucking adorable.

Jake took her in. "No, no, it's not like that."

"Sure it is. I hear it's a fuck-fest over there."

Jake took a sip of his coffee, keeping his head down.

"Honey, what are you trying to do!" Francesca put a hand over my mouth, and I quickly shooed it away.

"Nothing. Just stating the facts. I know the CEO there. Fred Barnby tells me exactly what goes on over those late lunches."

He choked on his coffee. "You know Frederick?"

"Of course, we share the same trainer."

He laughed nervously, giving me all the more reason to ring up my buddy after tonight and get a closer eye on Jakey boy.

The server appeared with the two plates. "So who's having what, or are we all sharing?"

I laughed. I couldn't help it.

Pepper threw me a scowl.

"We're all sharing," Francesca said, although she'd likely just have the garnish.

The server set the plates down in the middle of the table.

"Good choices, Francesca." Jake exclaimed, and fuck was it just me or had Jake and Francesca hit it off?

Not that I cared, I was more intent on watching Pepper. Body language was my specialty and all night, she had either moved into Jake or leaned away from him. There was no clearcut emotion all night. She'd be cold to him one minute, then warm as fur the next. It confused me. She confused me. She was a mystery, a goddamn riddle, and one that I couldn't evade no matter how hard I tried.

I drank the rest of my espresso and signaled the server to come around, handing her my American Express card.

"No, don't do that, Connor," Pepper finally spoke to me as the night was coming to an end.

"Don't argue with me, Pepper. It's done."

She looked at Jake for backup, but he shrugged. "He said don't argue with him. What can I do?"

She groaned in frustration. Well, sweetheart, join the fucking club. I had blue balls the size of Mount Etna.

Francesca waved away the server. "Let him pay. Connor is flush with cash, aren't you, darling?"

I glared at her. *Who the fuck says that?*

She blinked, then focused her attention on the table.

"So when's the wedding, Francesca? I bet you're both so excited?" She squealed, and I nearly threw up in my mouth. Francesca reached for my hand, and I closed my fingers around hers.

"We are so excited. I'm thinking of a wedding at the Plaza or maybe on Ellis Island? We'll have to book the best chef, and I've got Vera Wang on speed dial for my dress."

I hadn't given two seconds of thought about the wedding day, but I knew I fucking didn't want any of that. It sounded like the very opposite of what I wanted. She wanted lavish and large—a spectacle.

"Wow. Sounds like you're getting it all together, then?" Pepper smiled at Francesca, then briefly, her gaze met mine.

"I would want something small and intimate. With only my friends and loved ones around me. Strangers on my most important day isn't something I'd be too keen on, but that's just me."

My shoulders tensed as I watched her wrap a curl of black hair around her finger. I knew she did that when she was nervous.

*I knew everything about her body.*

"Me too," I admitted, drawing her gaze back up to mine. I inched forward in my seat. It made sense that Pepper wanted the same things as I did. We were compatible as fuck, and not only in the bedroom. I realized something that I knew all along —our relationship wasn't just physical.

She took her teeth to her lower lip, pressing down on it, her gaze lowering to the tablecloth. Intentionally, I extended my leg, finding hers under the table, and gently nudged against it. Startled, she jerked in her seat, pulling her leg swiftly away. The instant rejection bruised. I wasn't about to try again.

"No, no, we need to have the best wedding ever! Did you see the Paris Hilton wedding? So tacky, ours won't be like that. I'm thinking ice carvings and caviar."

*Oh fuck. No.* I didn't think I could go through with this. But what could I do to stop it?

Nothing. They had arranged this marriage forever. And I was the fucker with everything to lose and nothing to gain.

I gazed across at Pepper, willing her to give me something.

*Look up at me, please. Tell me this isn't just me. Let me see the chocolate browns stare into my soul. Show me you want this just as much as me, and I'll walk away. I'll walk away for you.*

"And that rock… geez, man, you know how to pick them!" Jake took my attention back to the table. I watched Francesca hold up her hand, showing off the diamond.

"She picked it actually from a tray of diamond rings."

"I did. I'm so lucky." She gasped, stroking the edges.

"How romantic," Pepper drawled. But with Jake and Francesca both admiring the ring, no one else seemed to hear it but me.

"And what are your intentions with Pepper here, Jake?"

"Oh my God, you sound like my father!" Pepper whipped her head up, her face flaming red from embarrassment.

"Well, if it were up to me, I'd propose to this girl here and now."

"What?" Both Pepper and I said while I nearly knocked over my tumbler of water.

Pepper stared at him in equal shock.

"We're just taking this slowly for the time being."

"For the time being?" I echoed her words.

*What does that mean? Was she fucking him?* If she weren't, it wouldn't be long until she completely let him in. Could I be pushing her toward him unknowingly? *Fuck, my head was spinning.*

"Well, if you insist, darls." He kissed her on the mouth. His lips on those lips my mouth brushed earlier.

She made no move to back away, and my shoulders braced upright. My heart pounded. I turned to Francesca and pulled her in, shoving my tongue down her throat in a heated kiss.

When I pulled away, I saw the shock on Francesca's face that quickly turned into satisfaction, like she'd finally won.

"Looks like everyone's in love around here," Francesca said breathlessly.

I looked over at Pepper, but her head was low, avoiding eye contact completely.

Well, if I hadn't sealed my fate prior, then that ought to confirm things for Pepper. She deserved to be happy, and if Jake was her happiness, I needed to concede. It was the last thing I wanted, but it was the only way. I needed her to be happy, and I was willing to pay the price for that. Pushing her toward Jake was the only way forward for both of us.

The server returned, handing my card back. "Thank you for coming to La Trattoria. Hope to see you all again soon."

"Not too soon," I mumbled, standing to pull out Francesca's chair.

\* \* \*

"Jake seems nice." Francesca's legs were close in the back seat of my ride.

"Nice? He's immature, don't you think?"

"Oh, I don't know. It's young love."

"I don't think they're in love."

"You seem very observant of the pair tonight. I know you're all friends, but you seemed to be a little standoffish toward both him and Pepper. Is there anything I should know?"

*Fuck.*

"No. If I'm short, it's because I have a lot on my plate. I agreed to take you out tonight. You were the one wanting to join another table, not me."

"You're right, but that kiss, I'd like more than that tonight," she said, rubbing her legs against me.

"Sorry, not tonight, Francesca… we're taking it slow, remember?"

Her hand hovered over the zipper of my pants.

"Don't get any ideas. The driver's taking you home."

She looked outside the window, presumably to check I was right.

"What the fuck, Connor?"

"Sorry, I have a ton of emails."

"Is this how it's going to be?"

## Lost Love

"We're both in a marriage that they forced us to be in. What did you expect?"

She huffed as the car came to a standstill.

"Did you ever imagine what life would be like if we weren't together?" I asked.

"What?" She smoothed down her blonde hair against her bony shoulder.

"Haven't you had boyfriends?"

"Of course, I've had many lovers."

"Have you ever been in love?"

"Why are you asking me this?" She narrowed her eyes. A flicker of sadness washed across her face. But with that frozen shit pumped into her skin, it was hard to tell if there was movement or I was just imagining it?

"Never mind," I said, reaching over and pushing open the car lever.

"You're being strange, Connor. I hope it's just because of the new role and the stress. Please tell me I have nothing to worry about."

I sucked in a breath. She was right. Our fate was sealed. It made no sense to dally in the world of what-ifs. That would only lead to disappointment and heartache.

"You've got nothing to worry about, Francesca." I kissed her on the cheek and said goodbye.

She walked outside without turning back.

*Get it together, Connor, before you lose it all.*

## 18

## PEPPER

"So Ari invited us to his grandmama's haute couture fall event. The afterparty is at Sky Deck. Ari knows everyone. Hot models, gorgeous women, it's going to be amazing and the hottest ticket in town!" Lourde said.

"I'll sit it out," I said, feeling conflicted after last night's dinner turned out to be a clusterfuck of emotions felt in just one kiss.

"You will not!" she protested down the line.

"You are coming... and Olivia, of course, we need to set her up with someone."

"I don't know," I said, painfully listening to my own whining.

"What is up? Are you still thinking about Mr. Hot Guy?"

*Every second of the day.* "No."

"You lie like the Pope, Pepper."

"Okay, well, maybe I am. But I'm also thinking about Jake."

"Well, isn't that a good thing?"

"Is it? I don't know. I'm so confused." I stared out the window of my apartment, wanting to feel anything but this.

"It depends what you're thinking?"

"We went out to dinner last night, and he was thirty minutes late again. There was no shred of remorse, either. Just excuse after excuse. I just doubt every word out of his mouth, and now I'm doubting we were even in love in the first place."

"Really? Oh, hun. I'm sorry you feel that way."

I picked off an invisible layer of lint on my activewear. "Yeah…"

"Why do I feel you're leaving something out here?"

"We also ran into Connor and Francesca at dinner… they ended up joining us at La Trattoria," I admitted, trying to sound as casual as possible and wanting to let Lourde in on my secret.

"Oh, excellent. Sounds like he's trying, at least. That will make Dad happy."

"What do you mean?"

"Everyone knows Francesca can be painful, especially Connor. They've been on again and off again for years."

"Do you think he is in love with her?" I asked, my stomach in a ball of knots, waiting for her to answer.

"No way. I don't think my brother is capable of love."

A deep and unwavering sadness replaced the instant relief I felt. A fuck was a fuck, and that's probably all we were, just like the many before me.

"He's never ever serious. You know Connor. He was like Barrett, a bachelor all his life."

"Well, Barrett is a changed man. Maybe it takes the right woman to change his ways."

Lourde laughed. "Ask any Manhattan woman, and I swear she knows someone that's slept with my brother."

"Ha." A nervous laugh escaped my lips. Hell, I knew that part was true. Still, it stung, thinking Connor had bedded half of Manhattan. But what right did I have over him?

"Pepper?"

"I'm here," I said, shaking my head.

"So, Thursday, Farrah Goldsmith's haute couture launch... I've got tickets for all of us... bring Jake if you want. I'll get him a ticket."

"Okay." I rolled my eyes, succumbing to her request.

She squealed so loudly that I had to pull the receiver away from my ear.

"You knew you'd get me to come along, didn't you?"

She laughed, and I growled, hanging up the phone with a smile.

\* \* \*

Thursday evening rolled around slowly. I hadn't seen Jake since our date, or rather, double date, where I kissed Connor in the bathroom stall. My hand dragged up to my bottom lip, remembering his lingering touch.

*Stop it.* I slapped my thigh. I'm going to give Jake my full, unbridled attention tonight. It's all or nothing, and I'm all in. Jake deserves that, and so does Francesca. I never intended to be the other woman, and clearly, this had turned out to be one fucked-up love triangle or rectangle. Heck, who knows what shape we were in?

"What are you doing in there?" Olivia said, banging on the toilet door.

"I'm coming, geez!"

I opened the door, and Olivia and Lourde were touching up their lip gloss in the mirror.

"It's about to start!" Lourde said, blotting on some cherry-red lip gloss.

"This dress, I don't know if it works." Olivia turned around, so her exposed back appeared in the mirror.

"Honey, you could be up there modeling with that dress

and those legs." I walked toward the sink and washed my hands.

"Says you, who is some kind of curvaceous specimen of the gods!"

I laughed hysterically.

"Olivia's right. How can someone show zero skin and steal the show?" Lourde nodded, eyeing me up and down.

I looked at my reflection. Wearing a lilac floor-length gown with long sleeves, the only skin on display was my face—hair pulled back into a chignon with some loose curls on either side of my face. The dress was tighter than a virgin on prom night. Thank God for Casey Jones, my relentless personal trainer. When I strive toward the finish line, she pushes me well past it.

"Does Jake love it?" Olivia asked, tugging at a wayward blond strand of hair and fixing it into place.

"He thinks I should show off my best assets."

"What, tits and ass?" Olivia stopped and stared at my reflection in the mirror, popping an eyebrow in disgust.

"Exactly."

"Such a guy." Lourde giggled. "They're all the same."

"Are they?" I dried my hands, then reached for my nude gloss stick, layering it on in one slick motion knowing Jake wouldn't kiss me with it on.

"Come on... we can't miss the start. I think The Weeknd is about to perform." Olivia motioned for the exit, and we filed out with the click of our heels against the tiled floor.

"Have you seen my brother? I thought he was coming tonight," Lourde whispered as we walked through the crowd, finding our seats in the front row.

"No," I said, hopeful he stayed away. *Where was Jake?* He was just sitting here a minute ago. Didn't he know the show was about to start?

"Oh my God, is that Anna Wintour?" Olivia gasped,

staring across from us at the rows of seats on either side of the catwalk.

Everything stopped. His dark eyes gravitated toward mine, and we connected like no one was watching. The room fell away, the noise, the people. It was just Connor and me. I tried to ignore the heat traveling up my body as his blues hit me square in the chest.

Wearing a sports blazer, open shirt, and chino pants, Connor could just as easily walk the show tonight as a model. Instead, he was sitting beside his beautiful fiancée, staring directly at me.

"Diane Von Furstenberg, Paris Hilton, Kylie Jenner, and Drake... they're all here."

"I never took you for a celeb hunter!" I commented while disengaging from Connor's steely gaze. When I leaned over Lourde, I saw that Olivia's face was lit up like a rainbow.

"Okay, okay, that's a cue to shut the hell up!" Olivia chuckled. "I'm so fangirling right now, though. Drake is my jam."

"Oh my God, you are beyond hysterical." Lourde threw a hand over her mouth, stifling a giggle.

"I think it's cute," I said. The music started, and the lights lowered. So did my focus across the room. Connor's stare was cold and hard as he focused on something behind me.

I craned my neck around. Wait, what the hell? Was that... that was him. There was no mistaking his royal blue jacket. Standing close to a beautiful, busty, and scantily clad woman, Jake touched her arm as they tossed their heads back in laughter.

"Jesus," I muttered under my breath.

If humiliation wasn't enough, an usher came to sit beside me, filling the empty seat just as The Weeknd performed their hit song, "Stargazer."

"What's wrong?" Lourde asked.

"Jake's flirting with someone behind us."

## Lost Love

She turned her head discreetly. "That's Scarlett Simpson. She's huge on OnlyFans."

"Fucking fabulous."

"Maybe he's just talking," Lourde said, with a pained expression on her porcelain face.

"Uh-huh, I'm sure they have a lot in common."

"Come on, let's just focus on the show. Don't worry about him."

I exhaled and watched the beautiful women walk down the aisle one after the other in the theme of Winter Wonderland. Feather, frills, and delicate lace graced the models in nude tones. The garments were stunning.

Between models, my gaze unwillingly found its way back to Connor. With Francesca's hand on his thigh, they looked every bit the Brad and Angelina of today. The *it* couple. I fumbled with my hands on my lap, feeling more insecure by the second.

*What was happening to me?* I wasn't insecure. I had my shit together. I had a boyfriend who I thought loved me and I loved him. I had the life I wanted. *I had.* I closed my eyes and let the music penetrate through my chest. When I opened, he was staring directly at me with piercing blues that could make the ice caps of Antarctica melt. Francesca whispered something in his ear, and I looked away. I couldn't bear the sight of them together. No matter how hard I tried to push my jealousy away, it was there like a code red.

Then I realized something.

I have nothing without Connor.

Oohs and ahhs echoed around the hall as the final model appeared in a showstopper. I watched as she floated down the catwalk, her long train and delicate lace gown absolutely stunning.

Applause echoed around the room as Farrah Goldstein appeared on stage. Her only grandson, Ari, clasped his arm in hers as his parents, Callum and Cindy, who'd I had the pleasure of meeting over the years, appeared by their side.

"How handsome does Ari look holding onto his grandmama?" Lourde squealed over the applause.

"Shame he is such an arrogant prick!" Olivia growled out.

"Did you hear that?" Lourde elbowed me.

"Fucking hunkholes," I agreed, regretting my decision to go out tonight.

"Right. Who's ready to party?" Lourde squealed. "Barrett just texted me, saying he's just arrived at Sky Deck. Let's go!"

## 19

## CONNOR

I had her in my sights from across the dimly lit room. Between the strutting models, she gazed up at me, a sadness in her eyes that was all too familiar. All I wanted was to take that pain away like she had for me, but our moment was gone when Francesca whispered in my ear, *"... if the models turned me on."*

*I mean, what the actual fuck.* I hadn't even noticed them with Pepper sitting across from me in that show-stopping dress. I was busy enough between eyeing her and noticing Jake chatting up a D-grade celebrity.

She deserved so much better than Jake. I knew his type. Hell, at his age, I was fucking anything in sight. But I had a backbone and fucking integrity. Cheating wasn't ever on my radar. And from what my buddy over at Manhattan General Hospital just told me, Jake was only a warning away from being fired for his lewd and suggestive comments toward the nursing staff.

He was walking all over her while pretending to give a fuck.

Well, not on my watch. She was being set up for disaster, round two. If he cheated once, he'd do it again. A leopard doesn't change his spots, and Jake's spots were tattooed on his skin. I was determined to tell her after the show and as soon as we could steal a moment together.

I don't know how, but Francesca had already dragged me out of the hall and into the waiting car. Sitting opposite me, she lifted her tits up. She'd handed me drink after drink, before the show and throughout, and now, in the short ride to the afterparty, I felt comfortably numb.

"Oh my God, that was amazing!" she cooed just as the car came to a halt, and she fell forward, landing in my lap. Looking down, my eyes met her tits.

*Fuck.* How I wish that was Pepper right now, between my thighs, burying her naturally perky tits into me.

"It's about time you looked at me like you wanted to fuck me," she said, sliding her hand down my chest.

I laughed. "If I didn't know you any better, I'd say you were trying to get me drunk to take advantage of me."

She leaned back, giving me pause to scan her body momentarily. I hated myself for doing so, knowing she was reveling in the attention, but my balls were so blue it hurt.

The driver opened the door, and she instantly rose. "Hubby, please… would I do that?"

I ground down on my teeth. "Don't call me that."

"Get used to it." She stepped out of the car to a crowd of flashing bulbs and posed.

*Great.*

I stepped out, smiled for a millisecond, then headed inside, leaving her to do what she did best.

Inside, the party was already in full swing. The celebrity DJ was spinning tunes in the corner while models and sports icons were at every turn. Ari was definitely in charge of the guest list. He knew everyone and had probably dated most of the models here already.

Themed lighting shone down on the bustling dance floor

where gorgeous people swayed and laughed. Coked-up models danced their bodies away, forgetting life and living in the now. Singers and celebrities were everywhere.

Sliding past people, I scanned the room, needing to find Pepper. Instead, I spotted Francesca in the corner chatting up the latest quarterback recruit to hit New York. It didn't bother me one bit. Actually, I felt oddly relieved.

I headed straight to the bar framed with feathers and neon lights with the couture brand.

"What can I get you, Mr. Diamond?"

"Whiskey neat."

"Coming right up." The bartender quickly went to work, pouring a hefty glass, then with one large square ice cube, placed it in front of me,

I looked down, noticing something peculiar about the ice cube in my drink. "What does that say?" I asked, looking at an inscription.

"Love."

"How cheesy and overrated as fuck."

The bartender laughed. "I know, right?"

I grabbed the glass and tipped it back, so the whiskey slid down the back of my throat. A sense of calm and numbness flowed through my body.

"Cheers, bud," I said, slamming it back down.

I pulled out a bill from my back pocket and handed it to him. "Grab a few for you tonight. Might make the night more bearable."

"Shit, thanks, man." He slid the bill into his pocket and smiled.

"Don't mention it," I said, turning around to find Ari and Magnus talking to a swath of models beside me.

"Look who's here!" Ari said, pulling me into a man hug.

"Hey, guys."

"Meet Chelsea and Franca," Magnus said, wrapping his arm around the tall blonde.

"Hey, great show," I lied. I really had seen none of it between eye-fucking Pepper and shooting bullets at Jake.

"Connor, we were so sad when we found out you were engaged." Chelsea pouted her sherbet pink lips.

"Were you now?" I said, noting the flirty infection in my tone. "Me too," I muttered.

Ari side-eyed me.

"Girls, would you excuse us for a minute?" Ari kissed the hands of the women one by one.

"Of course." They purred, taking their drinks and retreating to the next pile of money bags on offer.

Magnus turned, a scowl etched on his features. "What the fuck, man?" he scolded. "You know my divorce is done. I'm a free man as of today, and you turn them away?" He folded his arms over his chest and glared at Ari.

"Okay, spill, Connor. For weeks, you have been a grumpy prick," Ari said, completely ignoring Magnus.

"Well, Jesus, hello!" Magnus fumed. "Are we really doing this now at the after party of the year?"

"Doing what now? Have you guys been bitching about me like a bunch of schoolgirls on their period?"

"Call it what you want. But yes, Magnus, we are doing this now." Ari glared at Magnus, and he straightened, letting out a sigh.

*This should be good.*

"Great, I'm all ears," I said, reaching for whatever cocktail the server had on his silver tray.

"This drinking has started up again, and I think it has to do with Francesca."

"No shit," I said, taking a large sip of the fruity drink.

"Who are you fucking because it sure as shit isn't her."

"I don't kiss and tell… plus, it's none of your fucking business who I'm fucking."

"She complained to me the other night at dinner that you wouldn't touch her, so if you're not fucking her, then you're fucking someone else. And if I know you, you will get caught, and you will fuck up, and that's the end for you with Alfred."

"It's sooo nice that you care about me," I slurred out. "Maybe I should just fuck her then."

"Well, shit, man, if you don't, I'm sure the quarterback she's been chatting to will."

"Great, amazing, that would solve everything. Do you think we could coax them into fucking, film it, then the wedding's off?" I said, thinking I could be spared from my upcoming nuptials if she was the one to fuck things up instead of me for once.

Ari put his arm on my shoulder. "Man, are you hearing yourself? What the hell is going on?"

I sighed, walking over to the large ottoman seating and flopping down.

"I fucked someone. It was short-lived, and now I can't get her out of my head. She's like a migraine that just won't go away."

"But aren't migraines bad?" Magnus asked, sitting beside me.

"Shut the fuck up, Magnus," Ari snapped.

"She's pure sunshine," I confessed, staring into the crowd vacantly.

It was as though the clouds parted, and my focus came into view. Bodies dispersed, moving apart. There Pepper stood, her hands above her head, her body moving to the beat, her curves gliding to the rhythm in slow motion. I sucked in a breath. I knew her body intimately, every square inch and every curve.

Pepper turned, and our eyes met in an instant. She laid her hands down her body, and I swallowed hard. She was the sexiest woman here, and in a room full of models, that was saying something.

Closing her eyes, she let the music envelope her, and her hands trailed from her hair down the side of her body, tracing her curves like an artist sculpting a masterpiece.

"Oh hell, no." A voice beside me pulled me from my trance and the thickness pressing against my zipper.

"You were fucking Pepper?" Reluctantly, I pulled my eyes away from her only to find Ari staring at me in disbelief.

"Was. Am no longer."

"But you want to?"

I nodded. I didn't care if he knew or Magnus. She was an addiction I couldn't be without.

"Well, put her out of that head, Connor. Alfred made the deal. Your wagon is hitched to Francesca. The world knows it, and there's no going back, even if for a millisecond the thought had crossed your mind." Magnus stared at me, a stern look on his face.

"Don't you think I know all this?" I reached for my cocktail and painfully gulped it down.

"Fuck man, slow down."

"Why? My life's over anyway."

"Are you listening to yourself? Francesca is gorgeous," Magnus said. "You're rich, you've got a beautiful fiancée, one that is royalty, mind you... don't be so fucking ungrateful."

"Ungrateful?" I yelled over the music.

"Okay, chill, Connor. Magnus, shut the hell up, would you?" Ari said in a stern voice.

"If I have it all, then why do I feel dead inside? Why do I feel like I have nothing at all, like my world is on Groundhog's Day?" I slammed down my empty glass, heat scouring my chest. "Explain that to me, would you?"

"Because you're in love with Pepper," Ari said, squaring me with his matter-of-fact stare.

"No, I'm not,"

"Yes. You are." His voice was eerily confident.

I paused. *Is this what love felt like?* Like a stabbing need of wanting and thinking about the same person from waking up to closing my eyes at night?

"Fuck." I breathed out. The reality was a throat-punch sucking the breath from my lungs.

"You're fucked," Magnus offered.

"Sorry, Connor. I really am," Ari said, genuinely patting me on the back. "You're in no man's land."

"I know," I choked out. The cold, hard reality of the situation glared back at me.

"Do you think Alfred would…"

"You know the man, Ari. He's been on my back my entire life, waiting for this moment where he steps down and I step up. Grooming me for the role like his life depended on it."

Ari nodded. "What if you did the unthinkable?"

"And embarrass the family again?" Magnus asked. Both Ari and I turned to him. "What? I'm just trying to state the obvious." He held his hands up in surrender.

"I think those moments were my way of getting his attention from a father who just thought of me as an asset to his empire in years to come. Walking out on my destiny is not an option, although I wish it were because I'd jump at it without a parachute."

"There's my brother!" Lourde squealed.

"What do they say? Lemons equal lemonade. Squeeze the shit out of those lemons, my friend," Ari whispered as I watched Lourde and Barrett walk toward us and sit down. Behind them, Olivia, Pepper, and Jake sat down, joining everyone.

"Olivia, how nice to see you again!" Ari said in a weird, sarcastic tone.

"Isn't it?" she remarked, thrusting out a hip. "Perhaps we can debate how much cocaine is here tonight?"

"It's an integral part of every model's diet, but you wouldn't know that, would you?"

"Holy hell, stop it, you two!" Lourde burst out, but my mind was on the quiet Greek beauty in the corner with a man I despised next to her whispering something in her ear.

The server brought a bottle of bubbles to the table, and Ari stood up, opening it.

"Thank you all for coming to my grandmama's launch. I have an announcement to make. You all know I really do very little in my day, but I want to change that. I've decided to work with grandmama, and we are opening our very first flagship store right on Madison Avenue with me in charge of it."

"That's amazing, Ari. Congrats," Barrett said at the same time the cork flew off the champagne bottle, flying somewhere into the crowd.

"Congrats, man," I said momentarily, getting out of my own clusterfuck of a head to congratulate my dear friend.

* * *

I watched her on the dance floor. Her hips swayed side to side to the beat, her curves a deadly sin made for me. More than anything in the world, I wanted to disappear into the crowd, find her, and pull her close. I lifted the whiskey to my lips, imagining her body moving against mine and getting swept away in her arms. I closed my eyes shut, holding onto the thought. When I opened my eyes, hands moved from her waist and down, circling her ass.

*Jake.*

Drunk and irritated, I slammed down the rest of my whiskey and leaped off the wall, ready to rip his hands right off of her. But something stopped me. Instead, I paused and turned back around.

If, after what he'd done to her tonight, she was willing to stick with him, then she deserved him. My focus shifted, and in a flurry, I searched for Francesca. Finding her laughing and resting her hand on quarterback, Nick Stone, from the Giants didn't surprise me, nor did it bother me. I marched toward her, pushing and shoving people that got in my way. There was only one way to rid Pepper once and for all.

"Nick, stop it. You're too kind," I overheard Francesca purr. Out of the crowd, I appeared by her side and grabbed Francesca by the hand, steering her toward the exit.

I was done, done with all the bullshit, all the thinking that maybe, just maybe, Pepper and I had a shot. But by the way his hands slid down her body, I knew they were back together, and I was nothing to her.

"Whoa. Where are we going, Connor?" Francesca yelped out. She had to run behind me to keep up.

"Home, where I'm going to fuck you senselessly."

## 20

## PEPPER

I'd avoided Connor at the show, but it was his steely gaze during the catwalk event that was unavoidable, drawing me in like metal to a magnet.

At Sky Deck, the afterparty was magical. If only I could enjoy it. With Jake being more interested in chatting to everyone here and avoiding me, I honestly wondered why I brought him in the first place.

He claimed he wanted to be with me, wanted to make us work, but everything he did was the exact opposite. Being late on both of our dates, one I could understand but two, I had lingering doubts that something was amiss.

And with Lourde by my side, I watched him from a distance, chatting with yet another beautiful woman.

"Hey, you okay?" Lourde asked, placing a hand on my knee.

"Look at him, Lourde. What the hell? Is there something wrong with me?"

"You don't mean that." Olivia sat down next to me and handed me a glass of champagne. "I got you one too," she said, casting her eyes to where Jake was near the bar.

"Good thing you did. Otherwise, I'd still be waiting," I admitted. "Don't worry about me. I'll be fine," I said, determined not to let him spoil my evening.

Lourde and Olivia exchanged looks. "He seems awfully chatty with her," Olivia added. "Is she the same woman from the catwalk show?"

I shook my head. "I don't think so."

"No, that was the OnlyFans woman," Lourde said, craning her neck to get a better look.

"They're all models," Olivia said.

"Ari has the Rolodex for all the modeling agencies in New York," Lourde added.

Olivia blew her cheeks out in a puff. "Of course he does. He seems so different to his grandmama."

"Did you speak with Farrah Goldsmith?" Lourde inquired.

"Yes, just after the show. I actually saved her from tripping over."

"You did what?" I questioned.

"She fired the person who left the cable untapped on the floor. I was in the right spot at the right time. Then we got talking. She's so lovely. Her grandson, Ari, however, is an idiot."

"I hope you left out that part!" Lourde said.

"Of course, I didn't want to offend the woman."

"From what Connor's told me, I think she pretty much raised him too."

"How can that be? He's nothing like her?" Olivia questioned, very interested in Ari suddenly.

"Maybe because they're all hunkholes and arrogant, the lot of them," I said, taking in Connor, who stared at me from across the table where he sat with Ari and Magnus.

Anger burned behind my eyes. He shouldn't be looking at me like that. He had a fiancée. I had a boyfriend as far as he knew. But why did everything inside me light up with each stare he cast my way?

"Arrogant. Absolutely," Oliva agreed.

"But that arrogance makes them charming," Lourde said with a hint of a smile on her lips.

"Oh God." Olivia rolled her eyes.

"I'm with you, Liv."

"Hey, beautiful." Barrett appeared behind Lourde, bending down to kiss her on the forehead.

My heart kicked. Why couldn't I have that?

"Barrett." Lourde's face lit up like a virgin bloom.

He sat next to her and pulled her onto his lap, placing his lips on hers in a sweet embrace.

"You were just gone for like five minutes," Olivia said, rolling her eyes again.

I laughed. "Yeah, Jake's been gone all night." I shrugged.

"Ladies, when you find someone this special, a minute is a minute too long apart from one another."

"Oh God, it's so weird to hear my boss talk like that." Olivia laughed.

"That is so sweet," Lourde gushed, wrapping her hands to his cheeks and pulling him in for a deep kiss.

"So sweet," I echoed.

"Cheers to us, Pepper. Who needs men, huh?"

I lifted my champagne, clinking with her beer. "Absolutely."

Suddenly, my skin tingled with warmth. I didn't need to look to know he was staring. He was constant, like oxygen flooding my lungs.

\* \* \*

Dancing to the beat was the escape I needed from both men tonight. But closing my eyes only eradicated one. It did little to evade Connor. Imagining his lips tracing my body set me alight. The way my body responded to his stare sent tingles radiating up my legs and pooling between my thighs. But I just danced. Closing my eyes, I let the haze of alcohol warm me from the inside out. Then, out of nowhere, hands circled my waist, and I held my breath.

*Connor.*

*Please let it be him.*

The hands moved down to my ass, grasping it overtly. I opened my eyes. Blue eyes stared back at me. But they were the wrong shade. Jake smiled back at me, and I immediately jerked. "What are you doing?" I swatted his hand away, noticeably irritated.

"I'm touching my girl," he retorted. "Jesus, Pepper, are you on your period or something?"

My jaw clenched tight as anger coursed through my body.

He was mad, but fuck, so was I.

This couldn't work. Deep in my bones, I knew right at this moment that my heart belonged to someone else.

Jake moved away from the dance floor, and I turned back to where he sat.

But Connor wasn't there. I scanned the area for him. I needed to tell him how I felt.

It didn't make sense, none of it.

I left the dance floor and quickly floated in and out of people, trying to find him. Ari and Magnus were there, but he wasn't. I walked past the bar and toward the exit.

My heart raced, pounding like a metronome.

Whatever had become of me, Connor was more than just great sex. He was who I thought about day and night. Night and day. I didn't know how he felt about me, but I had to tell him. I had to be upfront and honest with myself.

I turned my head, looking left and right through the crowds of people

I laughed aloud when I spotted Jake talking to a model.

Fuck, all this time I'd wasted. Wasted on the wrong guy when all along, the right guy was in front of me.

With confidence at my back, I marched toward him and his wafer-thin model.

"Hey," she said.

"Pepper, I see you've come to your senses now?"

"Oh, you bet I have."

He stared at me curiously.

"We are done, Jake."

"What?"

"I tried to make us work, but the truth is, you're a boy who only thinks with his dick."

The model beside me laughed.

Jake flared his nostrils. "I never cheated on you, Pepper."

"So you say, but you cheat on me every day when you talk to women at the first sign of trouble between us. You've done that all throughout our relationship. You betrayed my trust too many times, and we're done."

"Wait," he said, reaching for my arm. "Are you serious, hun?" He appeared shocked and confused.

"You're a boy, Jake. I need a man." I gave him a steely look, his mouth slack-jawed.

"Damn girl," the model said.

I swatted his outstretched hand away and disappeared back into the crowd. My shoulders sat lower, my breath lighter.

*Now, where was Connor?*

The only area I hadn't looked at was the entrance. I quickly slid between people and headed that way.

With my heart in my chest and the crowd moving aside, I spotted the broad shoulders and muscular arms I'd memorized.

*Connor.*

Anticipation flooded me. Only a few more seconds until I told him how I felt. I didn't care that he was engaged. I knew it was just for show. He didn't love her. He…

*Lost Love*

I stopped suddenly, stretching out my hands to balance before falling forward.

He held the hand of Francesca, who was trailing behind him, and as the elevator doors opened, he pulled her inside. I quickly hid behind someone, so he wouldn't see me. As the doors closed, she threw her hands on him, her body against his as his hands circled her hips.

My heart stopped. He didn't push her away.

Tears pricked at the backs of my eyes.

I was too late.

## 21

## CONNOR

"Fuck." I tripped over something. My shin exploded with a bruising pain sending a throbbing ache up my leg.

I pushed the pain aside, determined to fuck my way out of despair. I was still going to fuck her, especially now that Pepper had clearly decided Jake was the man for her.

"Here's the light." Francesca giggled while finding the light switch. The fluorescent light stung my eyes. "You should fire your housekeeper for leaving that there." she tsked.

"Shh," I groaned out.

"Yes, sir."

I released my shin and grabbed her hand, pulling her into the bedroom.

Everything was blurry, hazy. My body ached with pain and frustration. "No!" I pushed aside the feeling of entrapment.

"No, what?" she asked, puzzled.

"Nothing," I murmured, not realizing I said it out loud.

I walked through the house, dragging her beside me. This was a bad idea. *Bad idea.*

Throwing open my bedroom door, I nearly lost my balance and fell forward.

"Wow, you are drunk." She giggled, and I steadied myself against the bed, looking up and noticing an impossibly large grin spread across her cheeks.

"I've been waiting for this for a long time," she said, slowly peeling off her dress down her shoulders and tossing it to the floor. Standing in nothing but a thong, Francesca stood in front of me. Ready and waiting.

Hot, beautiful, and fuckable. Every guy's wet dream, except mine.

*Get the fuck up and fuck her.*

She tilted her head to the side, gazing at me curiously.

"Do you need some help getting out of that?" She circled her fingers in my direction.

"I guess I do."

She walked over, her hand up to my lapel, I watched her try to undo my buttons, but she fumbled with her nails getting in the way.

"Dammit. I can't get it."

"Fuck it," I said, ripping off my shirt before I changed my mind. The buttons flicked like crickets onto the floor.

"Oooh la la," she purred, running her hands down the ridges and curves of my chest.

I closed my eyes at the touch. Slowly, Francesca ran her hands over every muscle, and I sucked in a breath. My discomfort slowly morphed into pleasure as soon as I brought Pepper into view.

I groaned out with her hands sinking lower to the inside of my belt buckle. Pepper's mocha eyes stared back at me. I couldn't wait any longer. I pulled her toward me, so she ground against the thickness in my pants.

My mouth hit her neck as I sucked on her lobe, biting and sucking down her jaw to her collarbone, where my mouth sunk into her skin.

Fingers touched beneath my belt buckle.

"Stop, Connor!" a voice boomed, breaking my trance. I opened my eyes and quickly jerked back at the sight of Francesca.

"What the fresh hell?" she squealed.

It took me a moment to understand the gravity of the situation. It was a voice I knew so well.

My gaze, although hazy, focused on the figure in the doorframe. "Ari, what the fuck?"

"Connor, you don't want this."

"What is going on?" Francesca straightened in nothing but her thong.

"Put something on, Francesca," Ari said, staring at Magnus, who was eye-fucking my fiancée.

*Not that I gave a fuck.*

Magnus stepped forward and picked up her dress, handing it to her. She snatched it from him and let out a quick disgusted snort.

"What the fuck? Get out of here," I yelled. "Ignore them, Francesca," I said, unzipping my pants.

"I will stand here and watch you if that's what it takes," Ari said.

"Fuck, I'm not into orgies, so I'm out," Magnus said, throwing his hands up in the air. "This was a bad idea."

Ari pulled him by the shoulder. "You're staying, Magnus."

"Can someone please explain to me what the hell is going on here?"

Ari turned up the lighting, the brightness making me squint and rendering me sightless for a minute. Once I regained my focus, I settled on the bed, Francesca making no move to get dressed.

"I'll tell you. He doesn't love you, Francesca. And this arrangement is wrong."

"Well, I know he doesn't love me. You came all this way to tell me that? This is an arrangement. Both families benefit from this." She threw her hand back and forth. "Maybe in time, who knows."

I was angry the boys barged in on us but even angrier with myself.

"This is how it is," I said in a whisper. "Alfred won't back out."

"So you want to back out?" Francesca turned to me, her face white, like a sheet.

"Of course, I want to back out. Don't you think we both deserve happiness?"

"What... wh... that is not possible, my daddy... yours..." She seemed flustered. After taking a deep breath, she composed herself. "We announced it to the world, Connor." Her voice was stern. There was no mistaking the warning in her tone.

Since I never took well to warnings, I stood up, taking her hand in mine. Maybe I couldn't have Pepper, but I knew I didn't want this. I didn't want this engagement with a woman I didn't love. I'd tasted love, and there was no going back. I'd rather be single and miserable knowing Pepper was happy than in a relationship with someone I couldn't bear.

"This isn't happening, Francesca."

She pulled her dress closer to her body, her bony shoulders caving inward.

"Look, maybe tonight was a mistake. I'm sorry, maybe I rushed things between us by oversupplying you with drinks."

I laughed. "Don't you think I knew what you were doing? I see everything, Francesca. It's over."

"That's not up to you to decide."

"Oh, but it is. It's my life. And for once, I'm grabbing it by the balls."

"That's it, Connor!" Ari said.

"Get the fuck out, you two."

Magnus laughed. "And just like that, the Connor of old is back."

"Is this funny?" Francesca flapped her dress out angrily before stepping into it and sliding it on.

"Not at all. This is our lives. You should be thanking me," I said honestly.

"Thank you? What do you think this will do to our family's reputation?"

"In time, news fades. But I am willing to look that saber-tooth tiger in the eye and wait and see what happens."

"This isn't over, Connor." She flicked her long mane of blonde hair behind her shoulders.

"Oh, but it is, sweetheart." I zipped my pants up, relief obliterating the haze I had moments ago.

She held her finger up to me, her teeth sheathed and staring me down. "Just wait."

"Are you threatening me, sweety?" I raised an eyebrow, slightly amused.

When she was about to speak, I put my hands up to her lips. They were so inflated they looked like a flight risk. "I don't take too kindly to threats, Francesca. Especially from whores like you."

"Connor!" Magnus shouted out.

"What?" She gasped, her mouth falling open. "How dare you. I'm the Duke's daughter. Wait until he hears what you called me!"

"How did the quarterback taste? I bet you gave him the royal treatment."

"What are you?" She stepped back.

"Seriously?" Ari roared out in laughter.

"I have eyes and ears everywhere. So when my fiancée disappears during the party, I make it my business to find out exactly where she is."

"You asshole!"

"I think you know the way out, Francesca."

She narrowed her eyes, her mouth slightly open, then turned her back and, like a tornado, left.

I stumbled back to my bed, my head hitting the pillow as I fell back.

What a fucking relief. But now, I had the task of telling Alfred the engagement was off. No mean feat, but I wouldn't back down, not now, not ever.

I closed my eyes, feeling the warmth of Pepper on my skin, the scent of her floral body wash, and the way one touch sent my heart hammering.

I shook my head.

*I was too late, wasn't I?*

## 22

## PEPPER

Ruffling down my black curls into a truly tangled mess, I stared at my reflection in my floor-length bedroom mirror. Red-rimmed and puffy eyes wouldn't be a great look at my lunch date with Olivia and Lourde. Trying to get out of it was futile. I'd tried. The texts I fired off in our group chat, feigning a headache, were met with, *"Drink a juice and down two Tylenol."* They were so empathetic.

I guess I couldn't blame them. They saw bullshit, and Lourde called me on it. At least they were coming uptown to Munch, my favorite bakery that happened to be on the street corner.

They picked Munch, so I wouldn't say no. No one ever says no to a sweet made by the talented and now renowned baker, Luca Coltres. *Oh God.* My mouth watered just thinking about the rich dark-chocolate croissant I was about to devour.

Slipping on my shoes, I gave myself one last glance in the mirror. The dress I picked out complimented my somber mood —black and fitted to just above the knee. I sighed. At least I had on my favorite pair of Mary Janes. Shoes made a girl feel better any time of day. And scanning the headlines this morning, I definitely needed a pick-me-up.

I grabbed my purse and headed out the door, pulling it shut behind me. As I descended the elevator and exited onto the busy street, the memory of the article still lingered.

Alarm had crossed Jake's face as he was photographed with his pants undone and a woman on her knees beside him. Well, if he wanted notoriety, he'd gotten it, his fifteen seconds of fame. He was the guy the OnlyFans girl blew at a Farrah Goldsmith's haute couture afterparty. He got everything he deserved.

It was something that probably should have surprised me, but really it didn't.

Deep down, I knew Jake wasn't the man for me, and I felt freer for breaking up with him last night. But the fact of the matter was, I was still upset. Not because Jake had his dick sucked by a whore, but because I was the one who pushed Connor away. For all his advances, heart-racing stares, and honesty, I'd pushed him toward Francesca.

By not wanting to be the other woman, I'd propelled him into the arms of a willing fiancée. But witnessing her push herself onto him in the elevator made my skin crawl and my heart thud dully in my chest. I'd left and cried my way home immediately after.

"There she is! I ordered you your croissant!" Lourde stood up, spotting me and calling me over to their table.

As usual, the place was swimming with people. Luca's expert dessert skills weren't a local secret any longer.

"Thanks, I could eat two of those. I'm so famished."

I slumped on the bench seat opposite them.

"Tell me what happened with Jake," Lourde said, extending her hand and placing it on top of mine. You disappeared and turned your phone off last night.

"Well, he got his dick sucked."

"Evidently." Olivia laughed. "But are you okay?" Olivia questioned, reaching for my arm.

"Honestly, I don't give a fuck about him. I broke up with him last night before it happened."

"You did? Is that why you just left like that? I tried coming after you because you looked like you'd just lost someone so close to you."

She squeezed my hand, and I pulled it away.

"Ah yeah, that's why."

I hated keeping secrets from Lourde, especially one as big as this, but I couldn't tell her now, could I?

I gazed up to find both Lourde and Olivia staring at me.

Lourde glanced between Olivia and me. "So if you're not upset about Jake, who are you pining over?"

She widened her eyes. "Wait, was Mr. One Night at the party last night? Is that what's going on here?"

A blush crept onto my cheeks. Fuck, I was the worst at keeping secrets. If I didn't want to tell her, my face was doing a better job for me.

"I knew it!" She hit the table with her hands.

The server appeared carrying a tray of food and drinks, and I was thankful for the interruption.

"Three chocolate croissants and espressos."

"Yes, yes, here, let me take that," Lourde said quickly, taking the entire tray from the server and placing it down on our table.

"Thank you," Olivia said.

The server realized he was interrupting us and turned on his heel.

Quickly, I grabbed the croissant, tearing off the end and shoving it in my mouth.

"No, no... you're telling us who he is and why you're so upset because it certainly is not over that jerk, Jake."

As slow as possible, I chewed the flaky pastry, the buttery

layers melting on my tongue. I swallowed down the last remaining piece of the pastry and reached for the rest when Lourde stopped me. "Speak."

"I don't think you're going to like what I have to say," I admitted sheepishly.

Olivia widened her eyes. "Oh shit, it's Connor, isn't it?"

Lourde flicked her head toward Olivia, who gave me a steely look.

"Good one," Lourde barked out in laughter, but when her focus landed back on me, I remained still, my heart pounding in my ear.

Her face turned serious. "Is this true?" Lourde swallowed down. "Have you been sleeping with my brother?"

"Not since he got engaged."

She removed her hand from mine and leaned back in her seat.

"I'm sorry, Lourde, it just happened."

"Oh my God." She remained stunned. "Did you know?" She turned to Olivia.

"No, but I saw the chemistry between them when we went out. It was undeniable."

I sucked in a breath, not realizing I'd stopped.

"I swear I ended it as soon as he got engaged to Francesca."

"And that's when you decided to make a go of it with Jake?" she asked, piecing together the jigsaw puzzle of my life over the last few weeks.

I nodded. "None of it matters anyway. It's done, he's in the past, and I wish him nothing but happiness with his new bride."

"Is that so?" She lifted her chin.

"Of course. I was friends with Connor for a very long time, and I hope we can continue to be friends." Although truth be told, I'd have to feign an illness to avoid his invitation to a wedding. No way could I attend that. Repeating vows with someone I knew he didn't love was just too heartbreaking to watch.

"I see." She sat, remaining silent.

"Say something, please, Lourde. You're my best friend. I don't want this to come between us."

I reached for her hand, grateful she didn't pull away.

"I'm weirded out, but I'll get over it."

"Oh, thank God." I blew out.

"Anyway, it wasn't like it was anything serious, right?"

I smiled. "No, no, of course not." My smile lowered into a line as I thought about losing him for good, the arms she threw around his neck. The dagger to my heart.

When I looked back up, Lourde was looking directly at me, curious in her expression.

"Anyway, so you had some news for me?" I asked, changing the subject.

"We do." Olivia piped up. "And it's a little exciting if I say so myself!"

"It is very exciting indeed." Lourde smiled at Olivia.

"Well, spill the beans then…"

"We are opening our own design studio," Olivia said.

"What? Seriously?"

"And Barrett? Does that mean you'll no longer work for him at his construction company?"

"We're working out the finer details with him, but he is very supportive of us doing our own thing."

"That's wonderful. You guys are such a dynamic team. You will kill it!"

"Well, we're under no illusion as it will be tough. We have zero clients and are starting from scratch," Olivia said, looking slightly fearful.

"Girl, you are so talented, your work speaks for itself," I gushed.

"I second that," Lourde said, patting Olivia on the back.

"So, do you have a name yet?"

"Bespoke Interiors," they both said at the same time.

"I love it," I admitted, so proud of my friends.

Conversation floated from the new company location to wedding plans for Lourde and Barrett's upcoming wedding as we sipped our piping hot espressos and ordered a few more pastries. During our conversation, I had moments where my mind drifted back to Connor. His words, his hands on my body, his generous heart. Blocking him out was futile. I guess he was just a memory I had to live with, and hopefully, one day, I'd wake up and never think of him again.

After paying, we said our goodbyes, and sheepishly, I placed my arms around Lourde, and she unexpectedly jerked me in for a huge hug.

"For what it's worth, I would rather have you as my sister-in-law than Francesca."

I laughed nervously. My heart pounded. Then emotion overcame me, and my eyes burned with unshed tears. *Oh God, she can't see me like this.*

"Okay, I got to run!" My voice came out strained as I released her and whipped around so she couldn't see my face.

"Pepper?" she yelled out, but I kept going. If she knew my tears were over her brother, she'd know what we had was much more than a fling.

With each step I took away from Lourde, the tears came like open floodgates streaming down my face.

## 23

# CONNOR

Alfred lurched past my assistant, marching toward my office. She didn't even try to stop him. Hell, I couldn't blame her. It would be the same as standing in front of a bull—he was that enraged.

*Well, good.*

*About time.*

Why wait any longer to do this?

Francesca had left with her tail between her legs last night, and I was surprised that word hadn't traveled sooner.

He barged into the office, throwing the door open. "What have you done, Connor?"

"Please, do come in." I shut my laptop, casting it to the side.

"The Duke called, screaming down the phone. Why did you tell Francesca the marriage is off? What sick twisted joke are you playing at?"

"I'm not playing. For once, I've got things right."

He stood against the desk with his hands on his hips, his face flushed with anger. "You need to call her and tell her you made a mistake."

I crossed my arms over my chest. "But I didn't make a mistake."

He clamped his jaw tight, then he swung his hands, pushing all the files off my desk, sending them crashing to the floor.

"Why are you doing this? Do you know what this means to the family name?"

"I don't care because I found love, and now I lost it."

Alfred shifted on the spot, taken aback by my candor.

"Yes, I found her, and now I can't have her. Problem is, I know what that tastes like, and I can't go into a loveless marriage knowing what I had."

He shifted from foot to foot. I'd never seen him like this before, so out of sorts.

"You're fucking out if you do this," he cautioned, regaining his composure.

"I don't care anymore, Alfred. You win. I don't want any part of it."

"That's bullshit, Connor. You want what I have. You want the notoriety. You want the recognition an empire brings."

"No. I don't. I've realized something. Maybe it's from years of watching you and Mom, or maybe most recently, it's from realizing my sister can have it all as she has with Barrett. But just maybe, I'm not cut out to be CEO. Just maybe my role in life is to be the best man I can be for someone else."

He stared at me for a moment before laughing. "You're willing to throw this all away for a girl?"

"She's not just any girl."

"I can't believe what I'm hearing. You know if you do this, the whole arrangement with Francesca's family, it will start a war. We've signed contracts. The relationship is binding."

I paused, fixing my glare on his. "And I thought you could get out of anything."

"Excuse me?"

"You heard me. Even if you can't get out of it, I'll wear it. I'd rather give it all up than be married to a woman I do not love. I'm worthy of love."

"And who is that you love?"

"Pepper Little."

"Oh fuck off."

"You wouldn't understand. It doesn't matter. She's back with Jake, and I've lost her for good." My heart stung, and he was laughing at my misfortune? "You are one cold-hearted son of a bitch," I said, balling my fists underneath the table.

"And they think we're mad." He raised his wiry eyebrows and offered a questioning gaze.

*The old man had lost his marbles.* "Who? What on earth are you talking about?"

He stood up. "Congratulations, son."

"You can fuck off if you're going to rub salt in the wound. I know I've lost and you've won."

"But, it's indeed the opposite."

"What are you talking about?"

"I lost my love a long time ago when I agreed to marry your mother."

He slipped his hand into his pocket and dug out his wallet. He slipped out a photo and looked adoringly at it, then let out a sigh.

"What the fuck are you talking about?"

He handed me the photo.

Torn and worn around the edges, a beautiful face stared back at me. It was the same photo I found in his wallet when I was a kid—the photo of a beautiful woman who wasn't my mom.

"I lost her because I followed my head and not my heart. You have done what no Diamond man has been able to do before you, Connor. You have followed your heart, and your heart leads to Pepper."

I threw the rest of the papers on my desk, shoving them to the floor. "And... what... was this some kind of test?"

He split into a smile. "Of sorts."

"You've been an asshole all my life." I spat out. My blood boiled with rage and confusion.

"Well, that was warranted."

I shot up and paced back and forth, trying to comprehend what the fuck was going on.

"Listen. I was hard on you because I knew one day you would have to make a decision. A decision to fuck it all off into the wind and marry someone because you were told to do just that or grow into the man I knew you could always be. The man I wish I were." He squeezed his eyes shut momentarily. "But you, son, you went against the grain. You choose to give all of this up for love. You are more courageous than me and your grandfather too."

He sat down, and I stopped pacing, taking him in. He was frailer and grayer than I'd remembered.

Did he really have that much regret on his shoulders? Is that what weighed him down all his life? My anger gave way to pity.

"Did you love her?" I pointed to the woman in the picture before handing it back to him.

"Leila." He gazed down at the picture of the woman adoringly.

"I left her for your mother. We had it all. We had plans. We were going to run away together, forget about it all, forget about your mother, who I was supposed to marry to help build the empire with her political ties."

"But you chose the money."

"I did, and there wasn't a day that went by that I didn't think about her and the life we could have had together."

I looked at my father, and for the first time in my life, I saw another man—a vulnerable man with a heart that had been hidden from me all these years.

"You're talking in the past tense."

"She died three years ago. She waited for me. She had waited for me all this time. And I never came for her. She never gave up on us, but I failed her."

He looked up, his eyes brimming with tears.

"I'm sorry, Dad," I said.

"That's the first time you've called me that in a long time." He blinked back the tears threatening to spill down his hollow cheeks.

"Well, that's the first time in a long time you've actually spoken to me like my father."

He nodded. There was no way I would forget how he treated me over the years, but today, for the first time, we had a common ground—love. Love makes you do strange things like risking an empire for a woman who is taken.

"So what now?" I asked.

He sucked in a breath. "Do you like running this company?"

"Surprisingly, I do. It's giving me a purpose. But what I don't like is a shadow."

"Understood. Well, things here will remain the same then."

"Is that so?"

"Yes, son, I think it's about time you take over from this old man and run this company with the same convictions you stand by and the same courage you just displayed to me."

"Seriously?"

"Seriously."

"And what about the Cavendish family, you know, losing it all."

"Please, we have the best lawyers in the country. There's no way I'm giving a cent to that snake."

I let out a dry laugh. "And mother?"

He shrugged. "We just go on existing. We're both so late in life, we probably couldn't get any better than each other anyway."

"I see." I rubbed the back of my neck. "I still don't know what just happened now."

He laughed and got up. He extended his hand, and I took it in mine.

"You're still an asshole." I clasped my hand around my father's, gripping it tightly.

"That's where you get it from. Now fuck off and get your girl."

"That ship has sailed. Pepper and Jake are together. She decided that clearly last night."

He laughed.

*Fucker.* I glared at him.

"For the president of a media empire, may I suggest you read our paper?"

"What for?" I scoured my office for the paper my assistant put there this morning, but everything was a mess of sheets on the floor from where we both threw papers earlier.

"Goodbye, son." He turned around, laughing.

"Wait…" I looked up, but all I saw was his bony back, sliding out the door as he waved to my assistant.

*What the hell was he talking about?*

My mind was buzzing. Like a dog to food, I pushed aside files and memos until I found the paper tossed to the side with loose sections.

Quickly, I flicked toward the back, scanning for something, some shred of hope that bloomed in my chest. I flicked the page, and a picture of Ari and his grandmother made me stop. I scrolled down to the bottom and the headline caught my eye immediately.

*OnlyFans Star Caught in a Compromising Position*

*Fuck me.*

A picture of a wide-eyed Jake with his pants around his ankles and her on her knees had been taken by a cell phone underneath the stall.

That lowlife piece of shit scum. What I wouldn't give to slam his face through sheetrock.

But as quickly as rage came, it went.

She was single, and so was I.

Anticipation tingled all over. She'd have to still want me. We were a match, a match that our grandkids could speak about one day of the love we shared.

She was the one I woke up thinking about and went to bed dreaming about.

She was the one, and I couldn't wait a second longer to tell her.

## 24

## PEPPER

All I wanted to do was binge-watch *Bridgerton* in my pajamas and eat baklava and ice cream. Instead, I was on my way up to Lourde's apartment.

It wasn't every day you announced the opening of your own interior design company, and I had a feeling great things were about to come their way. Their work spoke for itself, and with the recent media exposure of Barrett's townhouses, their name was front and center. I doubt they had to wait very long for the phone to start ringing. Going out on their own was a natural progression and a testament to their unique style. Like moving on from a broken heart was the natural progression for me.

So suck it up, I must. I exited the elevator doors and smoothed down my red dress. I quickly scanned the room for him but couldn't locate him. I hoped to hell he wasn't coming, but with Ari and Magnus here, he was bound to show up. Hell, it was his sister. I'd be a fool to think the Diamonds didn't stand by each other every step of the way.

So much for a small and quiet gathering. Lourde had invited half the goddamn block. The scent of sweet pickles and sharp cheeses invaded my senses and drew me further into her apartment.

Spotting Barrett, I lowered my gaze, finding him holding onto his fiancée, his hands holding her close in a protective and loving embrace.

*Damn, was it that hard to have what they had?*

Surrounded by Olivia and a group of people with familiar faces, I picked up a glass of champagne and walked toward them.

"Pepper!" Olivia squealed and rushed toward me, throwing her arms around me. "I'm so glad you're here. I felt like the third wheel with these two." She rolled her eyes toward an overly affectionate Lourde with Barrett.

"Wouldn't miss it. I'm so happy for you both. I brought you a gift for your new office," I held up the wrapped box just as Lourde and Barrett said hello.

"Oh, thank you!" Lourde said, pulling me tight. "I'm so excited for tonight," she whispered in my ear, and I looked up to find Barrett staring down at me.

"I'm excited too," I agreed, happy for my friend.

Olivia tore open the gold packaging. "What is it?"

She handed Lourde the unwrapped box. Opening the box, she pulled out one of two ceramic mugs.

They roared out in laughter.

"Oh, that's the best," Lourde exclaimed.

"Brilliant," Olivia echoed.

Written across the front were the words *Motherfucking CEO.*

"What's so funny?" His voice filtered past my heart, bellowing in my chest.

I didn't dare look up. I couldn't bear it, so I stared down at my black suede pumps. I fell silent as conversation swirled around me, and after a short while, I backed away slowly. I felt him turn to follow me, but Barrett called his name, and relief flooded my bones.

Mingling through the crowd, I quickly disappeared into Lourde's guest room, closing the door behind me and curling my shoulders into my body. Walking over to the opposite wall, I held my chest. It pounded against my ribcage. The pain rose in my throat.

I started pacing the room. If he was here, that meant Francesca was too, and as much as I thought I could suck it up, I was failing miserably.

A breeze hit me, then I realized it was the force of the door opening behind me.

"There you are." His voice was honey to my wound. I turned around, and Connor stared back at me. Cool eyes, blue shirt sleeves rolled up, and hair dusted to the side, he was a dream.

Just not mine anymore.

He closed the door behind him.

"What are you doing?" I asked, lowering my hand that was pinned against my chest.

He gazed at me up and down, the same stare that sent me alight with one look.

"Don't look at me like that, Connor."

"Like what?"

He stroked his chin, scanning my face and slowly my cleavage, then back up to meet my eyes.

"Like that!" I said, throwing my hands to my hips.

"Just because you know I'm single now does not change a thing between us. Now, move out of my way because we can't be seen together like this." I walked toward the door, but I shuffled past him when he didn't move.

"I wouldn't bother," he said.

Before opening it, I turned. "Bother with what?"

"We're locked in here."

"What?" I turned around and started jiggling with the knob, but it didn't unlock. "How?"

"If I'd offer a guess, I'd say Lourde."

I leaned against the door, unsure what was happening.

*Was this planned? If so, where was Francesca, and why was it so goddamn hot in here all of a sudden?*

He stepped forward, his body brushing against the fabric of my dress, and I let my imagination run wild at all the things I wanted him to do to me.

"You look beautiful, Pepper."

"I don't know what's going on, Connor, but I'm finding it hard to trust myself around you right now."

"Good," he breathed out, his lips brushing against my ear.

I pushed him away.

"Stop. I'm not going to be the other woman."

"I don't want you to be."

*How could he be so cruel?*

"Well, then it's settled," I said, willing away the burning tears that pricked in the back of my eyes.

I turned around, jiggling the knob again when his hand fell on mine and his body against my back. I stilled, my legs wavering beneath me.

"I broke it off with Francesca."

I turned around, my curly hair hitting him in the face.

He rubbed his eyes. "Ouch."

"You deserve that."

"Did you hear what I said?"

"Yes. So. You know you can't do that. You two are hitched. A done deal."

His blue eyes stared down into mine, his hands gently pressing against my forearms.

"I can't stop thinking about you, Pepper."

I shivered under his touch.

"It doesn't matter, Connor," I said in a strained voice. "You and Francesca…"

"Are done," he declared.

"I saw you two last night in the elevator. It didn't look done." I lifted my chin, squaring my shoulders in his direction.

"I went home with her because I saw Jake with his hands on your ass. I thought you two were together again, and it was like ingesting poison."

"On the dance floor?"

He nodded, clearly pained by the memory. The same pain I had when I witnessed her all over him in the elevator.

"That's when I grabbed Francesca and left, hell-bent on getting you out of my system."

"And did you?"

"I didn't fuck her. I couldn't. Nothing could erase the feelings I have for you."

My arms went slack, awash with relief at his revelation. Anticipation clawed in the depth of my belly. He tilted my chin up, and his eyes melted any resolve I had left.

"I can't let you be my lost love, Pepper."

"What..." I barely breathed out.

"I love you, Pepper Little."

He stroked the curve of my cheekbone, down to my lips, where his thumb lit every sensation in my body. "Tell me you feel the same. Tell me I'm not imagining..."

His gaze lifted from my lips to my eyes.

"Connor, shut up and kiss me."

With a slow and steady gait, he pulled my chin up to his, and I parted my lips, inviting him in. He drew me close and wrapped his arms around my waist, pulling me into his chest. He pressed his lips to mine and swept his tongue inside my mouth, gently at first, then with a bucking desperation that made me shudder with pleasure. I grew hot and feverish, feeling his thickness rub against me.

He groaned. "I can't wait any longer to have you, Pepper."

I sucked in my bottom lip. "Then don't."

## EPILOGUE
### ARI

Things were the way they should be. My two best friends were happy.

First Barrett and Lourde's engagement, and now Pepper and Connor were together.

Both unexpected world-shattering.

Magnus and I were the only single guys left in the hunkholes, the name Pepper had coined to describe the four of us.

I'd just thrown the epic afterparty at Sky Deck, and now I had my first meeting with my grandmama about opening up the new Farrah Goldsmith flagship store on Madison Avenue.

I stood as soon as I spotted Grandmama entering the French café. I walked through the crowds and tables with little walkways toward her. "Grandmama, morning,"

"Aristotle, my grandson." She held her bony arthritic hands to my face, rubbing the stubble on my cheeks—the same way she'd been greeting me for years. I looped her hand in mine as we walked slowly toward our corner table. "What a roaring success the show was last night."

"You outdid yourself again, Grandmama," I commented, so proud of the woman who practically raised me.

"Sit, please." I held out the chair for her as she steadied herself and lowered into it, setting her wooden cane against the marble counter.

"I've already ordered your tea. It should be coming any moment."

"Excellent. Now down to business." She clapped her hands together and rubbed them back and forth. "We have loads to do."

"Absolutely. I cannot wait." I leaned forward in my chair, unable to contain my excitement for what lay ahead.

"We have the site, we need to hire the interior people, and I have just the team."

"You do?" I asked curiously, wondering if she ever rested in her late age.

"Lourde Diamond and her friend, Olivia, started a company called Bespoke Interiors."

I stilled in my seat.

*Olivia? I had to work with Olivia?*

"No, Grandmama." A vein ticked in my neck. Olivia was my arch enemy. "Each time we've met, we have come to blows. At the charity ball, dinners, and now my latest party, she's so infuriating, arguing with me on any little thing. It won't work."

"Perfect, we need someone able to challenge you." Grandmama smirked into a gleeful smile. Was she enjoying this?

"It's not a good idea," I cautioned, unsure how I'd get through a single day working beside the woman I loathed.

"It's done," she warned, a finality to her tone I'd heard many times before.

*Great.*

She looked at me curiously, and I let out a sigh. "She's a thorn in my side, Grandmama."

"A pretty one at that," she countered.

My mind wandered to her at the party at Sky Deck. Pretty, yes. Sexy perhaps. But there was absolutely no way I'd ever consider her as anything other than an annoying thorn in my side.

"You'll be just fine, Aristotle. You'll begin Monday morning."

*Well fuck.*

## ALSO BY MISSY WALKER

### Sassy Seaview Series

Trusting a Rockstar

Return to Home

Beyond Melting

### Elite Men of Manhattan Series

Forbidden Lust

Forbidden Love

Lost Love

Missing Love - Preorder for October

### Fairbank Series

### (coming soon)

Unloveable #1

Untangled #2

**Join Missy's Club**
Hear about exclusive book releases, teasers and box sets before anyone else.

Sign up to her newsletter here:
www.authormissywalker.com

Become part of Missy's Facebook Crew
www.facebook.com/AuthorMissyWalker

# ACKNOWLEDGMENTS

This one is to the Hubster.

Your support is endless. Without you I wouldn't have the time to craft these stories that play out in my mind, and make me so happy.

For more than twenty years you've tested me, supported me and loved me like every woman should be loved.

This is all for you x

## ABOUT THE AUTHOR

Missy is an Australian author who writes kissing books with equal parts angst and steam. Stories about billionaires, forbidden romance, and second chances roll around in her mind probably more than they ought to.

When she's not writing, she's taking care of her two daughters and doting husband and conjuring up her next saucy plot.

Inspired by the acreage she lives on, Missy regularly distracts herself by visiting her orchard, baking naughty but delicious foods, and socialising with her girl squad.

Then there's her overweight cat Charlie, chickens, rabbit and bees if she needed another excuse to pass the time.

If you like Missy Walker's books, consider leaving a review and following her here:

tiktok.com/@authormissywalker
instagram.com/missywalkerauthor
facebook.com/AuthorMissyWalker
www.amazon.com/Missy-Walker
bookbub.com/profile/missy-walker

Printed in Great Britain
by Amazon